Bella Broomstick

SCHOOL SPELLS

Bella Broomstick

SCHOOL SPELLS

LOU KUENZLER

ILLUSTRATED BY
KYAN CHENG

SCHOLASTIC

Scholastic Children's Books
An imprint of Scholastic Ltd
Euston House, 24 Eversholt Street, London, NW1 1DB, UK
Registered office: Westfield Road, Southam, Warwickshire, CV47 0RA
SCHOLASTIC and associated logos are trademarks and/or
registered trademarks of Scholastic Inc.

First published in the UK by Scholastic Ltd, 2016

ISBN 978 1407 15796 2

A CIP catalogue record for this book
is available from the British Library.

Printed by CPI Group (UK) Ltd, Croydon, CR0 4YY
Papers used by Scholastic Children's Books are made
from wood grown in sustainable forests.

1 3 5 7 9 10 8 6 4 2

This is a work of fiction. Names, characters, places, incidents
and dialogues are products of the author's imagination or are used
fictitiously. Any resemblance to actual people, living or dead,
events or locales is entirely coincidental.

www.scholastic.co.uk

To my spellbinding girls

\- LK

Chapter One

My foster parents dropped me at Person school for the very first time.

"Have a brilliant day, Bella!" they said as we found my new classroom at Merrymeet Primary.

My cuddly foster-mum, Aunty Rose, flung her arms round me and gave me a huge, squeezy hug. Sometimes she smells of strawberries. This morning it was peaches and cream... I don't think I'll ever get used to how delicious Person lotions and potions can smell. I used to live with my mean witchy Aunt Hemlock in the Magic Realm. Her idea of a gorgeous potion was a grow-your-own-wart cream!

"Don't get up to any mischief, Bella!" My foster-dad, Uncle Martin, held up his hand for a high five and then wiggled his fingers like we always do.

"See you later," I said, trying to sound brave as my new teacher, Miss Marker, showed me to my seat. The last time I had been in a classroom it was to sit the entrance exam for Creepy Castle School for Witches and Wizards. I nearly exploded the whole dungeon by mistake.

At least there won't be any magic here at Merrymeet Primary, I thought. But as Miss Marker finished taking the register, she set us a different kind of task.

"I want you to write a story, Indigo Class," she said, pointing to the title on the board.

What I Did in My Summer Holidays

Tumbling terrapins! What was I supposed to write about? Could I describe the time Aunt Hemlock took me and her magic chameleon, Wane, to pick fungus in the deep, dark Forest of Doom?

Or the time I was taking a bath in the swamp and accidentally washed my face with a toad?

Perhaps not! Nobody here in the Person World is even supposed to know I am a witch.

After ten minutes, all I had managed to write was my name.

I twiddled my fluffy pink flamingo pen. I was so busy thinking what to say, I didn't even notice I had started to doodle on the empty page...

Bella Broomstick

"What's that?" Piers Seymour, the nosy boy who lives next door to me, peered over from his table.

"Nothing!" I said, quickly screwing the paper into a ball. Aunt Hemlock says if any Persons find out I really am a witch, they'll boil me in a pot. Or worse, she'll drag me back to the Magic Realm to live with her.

I reached for a fresh sheet of paper. But it was hopeless. I still couldn't think where to start my story.

"Finished, miss!" Piers Seymour's arm shot up in the air. "Shall I check through for spelling mistakes and then copy my story out in neat?"

"Good boy," beamed Miss Marker. She looked so pleased; I wished I could make her smile like that. But, after living next door to Piers for just one week, I knew he wasn't really a good boy at all. He was the sort of Person who bullied kittens and stamped on ladybirds just for fun.

"I've done two whole sides, miss!" Piers boasted, waving his pages in the air. "And Bella hasn't written a thing."

"Oh dear." Miss Marker frowned. But, before she could say anything else, a girl with long pigtails flying out behind her skidded through the classroom door.

"Sorry, miss. The bus was late," she said, sliding into the spare seat beside me with a friendly smile. I recognized her at once as the same girl I had seen on my way home from town a few days earlier. She had been singing songs with her little sister and I had hoped at once that we could be friends. I didn't know her name, though, as she had missed the morning register. I would have to wait to find out.

Piers was still smirking at my empty page.

"What are you going to write, Bella Broomstick – or should I say Bella *Broomthick?*" he hissed under his breath. I know he thought he was being very funny, but it's not the first time I've heard that Bella *Broomthick* joke. Mean young witches and wizards used to say it all the time when my spells went wrong in the Magic Realm.

"Don't pay any attention to Piers. I bet your story will be brilliant," whispered the smiley girl as we all got back to work.

"But what if I can't think of anything to write?" I asked in a low voice.

"Then make it up! I always do," she giggled. I could see she had already written three sentences of her own.

I certainly wasn't going to write about the day I failed the exam to get into Creepy Castle School for Witches and Wizards and made the examiner so cross his head fell off.

That was when Aunt Hemlock had banished me to the Person World. She'd cast a spell on Aunty Rose and Uncle Martin so they would let me live with them (even though they are not my real aunt and uncle – and they have no idea that I am a witch, of course), and—

"Crazy comets!" I gasped out loud. "That's where I'll start my story."

I began to write as fast as I could.

What I Did in My Summer Holidays

I came to live in
Honeysuckle Cottage
when Aunty Rose
and Uncle Martin
agreed to foster me.
They are the nicest,
kindest Persons in
the whole world.

They even let me adopt
a little grey kitten
called Rascal.

I have my own bedroom with
roses on the wallpaper and
Aunty Rose took me shopping
at the Sellwell Department Store

in town. She brought me lots
of lovely new clothes and
my fluffy flamingo pen.

"Just so long as no one ever finds out this pen is really a wand," I thought, looking up and smiling at the class goldfish that was swimming round in its little glass bowl. My life had changed so much since I'd left the Magic Realm at the end of the summer holidays. All I wanted now was to be a normal, non-magic Person and make some new friends at school.

"Don't look so worried!" The little goldfish pressed his lips up against the glass. "You'll be fine!" he mouthed, talking to me in Goldfish Gulp (which is a language I understand quite well).

"Thank you!" I mouthed, answering in perfect Goldfish Gulp too.

Chapter Two

"You were talking to the fish!"

Piers Seymour followed me across the playground at break.

"No I wasn't!" I fibbed.

Piers clicked his fingers. "Over here, Knox." A boy as big as a troll blocked my path.

"I don't speak fish..." I said as Knox and Piers hemmed me in between them. That's not true, actually. Animal languages are the only thing I have ever been any good at. Goldfish Gulp is quite easy, and I even speak a bit of Shark.

But I knew better than to tell Piers and his giant henchman friend that I can talk to *cats* and *rats* and *bats* as well.

That sort of thing just isn't normal in the Person World.

"Are you all right there?" The smiley girl from my table came skipping towards us. She was wearing the same green Merrymeet Primary School sweatshirt as everybody else ... but she had also put on a sparkly gold top hat. She looked by far the most exciting Person in the whole playground. "I'm Esme, by the way," she said, swerving past Piers and ducking under Knox's arm so that they had to step out of my way.

"And I'm Bella." I smiled gratefully as she grabbed my hand and we dashed towards the climbing frame together.

"Actually, my real name is Esmerelda. But nobody ever calls me that," she grinned, hanging upside down from the bars. "It is after a girl in a funny old fairy tale called *The Hunchback of Notre-Dame*."

"And my real name is Belladonna!" I confessed. "After a deadly poisonous plant."

"Oh dear. I thought mine was bad!" Esme snorted, making such a funny sound that I had to laugh too. "Well that's it!" she smiled. "Now you've told me your secret we'll have to be friends."

"Blazing bats! I'd love that," I grinned, thinking of all the brilliant things I could do with a real Person friend.

Eating delicious puddings

Shopping (especially at Sellwell Department Store)

Dancing

"My mum owns Merrymeet Bookshop – or at least she used to," Esme explained. "She loves old stories so much she gave us all fairy-tale names. My baby brother is Jack. But he's so tiny we just call him 'Bean' like Jack and the Beanstalk. And my little sister is—"

"Gretel – like Hansel and Gretel." I smiled. "I met her once at the windmill where you live."

"Of course. You gave our little grey

kitten a new home," she said.

I was about to tell her how well Rascal had settled in when Esme swung down from the bars and clapped her hands with excitement.

"Do you want to see some magic?" she asked.

"Magic?" I nearly fell off the climbing frame. "Are you a witch like m—" I stopped myself just in time as she lifted up the top hat and pulled a toy wand out from underneath it.

"Ladies and gentlemen, boys and girls," she called in a deep, mysterious voice as the class gathered round. "Watch carefully... I will make a rabbit appear from this hat!"

I should have guessed... Esme wasn't

going to do real magic like mine. It was just a trick. I had seen Persons on television doing the same sort of thing.

"Abracadabra!" Esme tapped the top hat with her plastic wand. "Ta-da!" she cheered. But the hat was empty.

No rabbit at all.

Esme's face fell. "I've been practising that trick all summer," she sighed.

"What a loser!" sneered Piers.

My fingers twitched. If only I could wave my fluffy pink pen-wand and make a rabbit magically appear inside Esme's sparkly hat... That would keep Piers quiet. But I didn't dare risk it. I am not supposed to do any magic at all in the Person World.

"Look! There's something poking out of Esme's pocket," laughed Piers.

"Oh dear! You weren't meant to see

that!" said Esme, spinning round.

But it was too late. Piers had already snatched the little toy bunny she was trying to hide.

"It's not even a real rabbit!" he laughed, holding it up by its long yellow ears.

My wand twitched furiously.

"Just give Esme back her toy," said a dark-haired girl called Zoe who sat at our table in class.

"I want to see the trick," agreed Zoe's twin brother, Zac.

"Fine!" Piers glanced around. The teachers were huddled together drinking coffee by the staffroom door. None of them were looking our way. "Go and get it then!" he laughed, kicking the little toy across the playground.

"Don't! That's Bunnykins. He belongs to my baby brother," cried Esme.

"Oh. Ickle Bunnykins!" Piers taunted her.

I dashed forward and picked up the little fluffy rabbit. He had mud all down one yellow ear.

"Poor thing!" chorused a group of girls.

"What's all the fuss about?" sneered Piers. "The stupid toy is probably from a jumble sale, just like everything Esme's family owns. They couldn't even afford to pay their rent. That's why my dad threw them out of their flat. Now they live in a mouldy old windmill." He snatched her gold top hat and put it on his head.

"Look at me! My name's Esme Lee," he

mimicked. "And I'm the worst magician in the world..."

That did it! My wand twitched again.

I had to do something to stop Piers bullying my new friend. What harm could a teeny-tiny bit of magic do?

Chapter Three

Esme grabbed her hat from Piers. She threw her head back, bravely trying to ignore the horrible things he was saying. But I could see tears in the corners of her big blue eyes.

"Have another go at your trick. I bet it will work this time," I said.

"Do you really think so?" Esme asked.

"Of course." I nodded encouragingly, sure that with a little secret magic I could help her out.

"Roll up, roll up!" she cried, really getting into character as some of the class gathered around again.

I hovered at the back of the group where nobody could see me.

"I am the great and mysterious conjurer Esmerelda," said Esme. She was brilliant at acting. "Prepare to be amazed..."

"Ha! It'll never work," Piers laughed. But the twins were cheering and Knox's eyes were as big as saucers.

I whispered under my breath:

Make a rabbit appear in the hat ...
Make him small and cute and ...
Er ...
... very fat!

It wasn't a brilliant poem. But it's always important to at least try and rhyme when you're saying a proper spell.

"Abracadabra!" said Esme, like the conjurers I had seen on telly-vision. (No real witch or wizard would ever say that.)

The moment she tapped the golden hat with her plastic wand, I waved my wand too.

POOF!

There was a puff of purple smoke.

"Wow!" cried all the children, staring at Esme in amazement.

The smallest, cutest, FATTEST rabbit I had ever seen popped his head up over the brim of the hat.

"Spinning spell books! It worked... It really worked!" I gasped, slipping my wand safely behind my ear.

Esme was looking more surprised than anybody. But the whole of Indigo Class were clapping and cheering.

All except for Piers, of course.

"It's only another silly toy or something!" he said, pushing everybody out of the way and peering into the hat. The greedy little rabbit must have been hungry. Perhaps he thought Piers's long skinny nose was a carrot because. . .

Chomp!

He stuck out his sharp front teeth and took a good hard bite.

"YOUCH!" Piers leapt in the air, holding the end of his nose.

Everyone roared with laughter.

"What an incredible trick!" they cried.

"That's definitely a real rabbit," said Zac.

"With real teeth," agreed Zoe.

"I'll get you for this, Esme Lee!" said Piers furiously. There were real teeth marks on the end of his nose.

Even Malinda and Fay, the two mean-looking girls who shared a table with Piers, were clapping. "It's such a cute bunny," they cried.

Only Knox was quiet. The enormous boy bent down, gently lifting the little fat rabbit out of the hat where Piers had dropped it on the ground.

"Are you all right, bunny?" he whispered, scooping the fluffy creature on to his giant palm.

"We should call him Nibbles, after the greedy way he tried to eat Piers's nose," I said. Then I leant down close to the rabbit's long twitching ears. "Welcome to Merrymeet Village, my magical friend," I whispered.

I don't know if it was the enormous size of Knox's hands or the shock of hearing someone talk to him in his own Rabbit language, but Nibbles took one look at us both and leapt off Knox's palm. He shot away across the playground, burrowed under a gap in the school gate, and hopped away along the lane as fast as his floppy feet would carry him.

"Perhaps he's a wild rabbit. I bet he's heading for the village green," said Zoe. "That would be a lovely place for a bunny to live."

"Look!" cried Esme as we all peered through the railings. "His tail has got a magic star on it."

Sure enough, as the little rabbit disappeared around the corner, I saw a perfect black star shape right in the middle of his fluffy white tail.

Chapter Four

As the bell rang for the end of break, Piers blocked the classroom door.

"I don't know how you managed that stupid trick, Esme Lee. But you and your fat little rabbit made a fool of me," he said.

His nose was still bright red from where Nibbles had nipped him. I noticed people were giggling behind the bully's back... But now the excitement was over, no one was brave enough to laugh out loud.

"Big mistake!" hissed Piers, almost spitting in Esme's face. "My dad will make sure you and your scruffy little family never find a home in this village ever again!"

"Can he really do that?" I asked, grabbing Esme's arm as Piers stormed into the classroom.

"Probably! Mr Seymour is the richest, most powerful man in Merrymeet," she said. "Piers is right. He already threw us out of our flat and closed down Mum's bookshop."

"Whispering weasels!" This was a disaster. When I waved my wand, I had only meant to help Esme with her trick. I thought if a real rabbit appeared it would stop Piers teasing her. Instead greedy little Nibbles had bitten him. Now Piers was hopping mad . . . and he thought it was all Esme's fault.

"What I don't understand is how Nibbles

got into my hat in the first place," said Esme, shaking her head. "My trick was only supposed to use Bunnykins." She pointed to the fluffy toy rabbit still poking out of her back pocket.

"Umm . . . isn't the lesson about to start?" I said, trying to change the subject. My heart was pounding like a bunny's back foot. If Esme found out I had used real magic to interfere with her trick, she'd never want to be my friend. She'd know it was my fault she was in so much trouble with Piers and his powerful family.

Luckily, Miss Marker clapped her hands. "Settle down," she said as everyone hurried to their seats.

"As you will notice," Miss Marker continued, "all the tables in this classroom are named after different planets."

"Ours is Mercury. I'm so glad you're on

the same table as me," said Esme, giving me such a friendly smile, I was sure she had no idea the naughty bunny was all my fault.

"Me too!" I whispered. I was so thrilled to be on silver-painted Mercury with Esme and the twins that I didn't even mind that Piers and Knox were right beside us. They were on bright red Mars with Malinda and Fay, the two spiteful-looking girls who kept whispering about everyone else in the class.

I saw them pointing at me and Esme, before they turned away and started to giggle.

Miss Marker clapped her hands and we all fell quiet again. "I wonder if anyone knows who first gave the planets their names?" she asked.

Zoe put her hand up. "Was it the Romans, miss? I think they named the planets after their gods."

"That's right. A gold star for Mercury table," smiled Miss Marker, putting a shiny sticker on our chart.

Piers and the Mars gang groaned.

"Mercury was the Roman messenger god," said Zac excitedly. "He had winged sandals so that he could fly through the air."

Wobbling wizards. That sounds even harder than riding a broomstick, I thought.

"Well done, Zac," said Miss Marker,

putting another sticker on our chart. "And Mars was the god of war."

"Cool!" Piers glared at us from the red table. "We'll fight you all . . . especially you, Esme Lee!" he hissed under his breath. But as soon as Miss Marker turned round, he smiled sweetly, as if he wanted a hundred gold stars for being nice to teachers. "Are the Romans going to be our special topic this term, miss?" he asked.

"That's right!" Miss Marker smiled.

"She has no idea what Piers is really like," whispered Esme. "If she did, she'd be furious. She is strict but very fair."

Miss Marker clicked her computer and a picture of funny-looking Persons dressed up in sheets and sandals appeared on the whiteboard. I don't think I'll ever get used to the way things like that can happen without using magic.

"For homework, I want you to split into pairs and find out one particularly interesting fact about the Romans," she said.

"Cool!" Zoe smiled at her twin brother. "We've got some great history books at home."

"Can I be your partner, Bella?" asked Esme. "You can come for tea at the windmill if you like."

Tea? With a real Person friend? On my very first day of school? Suddenly I forgot about Piers Seymour and his horrible threats. "Yes please!" I grinned.

But Esme leant close. "Good," she whispered very quietly. "Then you can tell me how you did that magic spell!"

"Magic spell. . .?" I froze with my mouth

wide open like the class goldfish. "Wh...
What magic spell?" I gulped.

Esme's blue eyes twinkled as she looked
straight at me.

"The rabbit in the hat spell, of course!"
she said. "I know it was you, Bella. You're
a witch aren't you? A real one — not just
pretend."

I stared back at her and swallowed hard.

"Yes!" I whispered. My secret was out.

Chapter Five

Esme was jumping up and down in the lunch queue.

"You're a witch! A real, live witch!"

"Shhh," I hissed, looking over my shoulder. She was so excited I thought she might tell the whole dinner hall. "No one must ever find out."

"OK. But it's just so brilliant! Can you really do spells and ride a broomstick and make potions?" she asked.

"I'm not very good at magic yet. But I am getting better since I've had my new pink wand," I whispered, pointing to my fluffy flamingo pen, which was tucked behind my ear as usual.

"You made Nibbles and he's adorable," said Esme as we reached the food counter. "I think you're amazing!" She didn't even seem to mind that I had got her into so much trouble with Piers. "By the way, don't have the Brussels sprouts," she warned me. But it was too late. The dinner lady had already emptied a heaped spoonful of soggy green vegetables on to my plate. They looked even worse than the frog fritters Aunt Hemlock used to serve.

"Mind you finish everything up," said the dinner lady as Esme quickly chose a big helping of pizza and chips. "That's the rule at Merrymeet. Nice clean plates!"

"I've never tried sprouts. But I'm sure they can't be that bad," I said, following Esme to a table. That was before I took my first bite...

TEN WORST THINGS I HAVE EVER EATEN

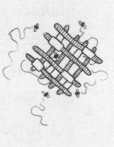

10. Snail pie
9. Slug sandwich
8. Slime shake
7. Toad-in-the-hole (with real toad)
6. Frogspawn jelly
5. Jellyfish jelly
4. Sour milk sundae
3. Worm waffles
2. Aunt Hemlock's famous frog fritters
1. Soggy school Brussels sprouts

By the time we finally left the dinner hall, my tummy was gurgling and burbling like a bubbling cauldron. Brussels sprouts definitely didn't agree with me.

"Ew!" squealed Malinda as my belly rumbled louder than a grumbling troll.

"That's disgusting!" called out Fay.

Esme led me away to a quiet corner of the playground. I took my mind off my tummy by telling her everything I could think of about being a witch.

We hadn't been talking for long when a crowd gathered.

"Please make another rabbit appear, Esme. Nibbles was so cute," begged a girl called Lexie.

"At least tell us how you did the trick," said her friend Keeley.

I froze as Esme looked towards me. For a moment I was sure she was going to give me away. But she bowed with a wave of her gold top hat. "The Great and Mysterious Esmerelda never reveals her secrets," she said.

"Bravo!" laughed the twins.

Esme was so brilliant at playing her character; she really did seem like a mysterious magician. For a moment, I almost forgot it was actually me who had put the magic rabbit in the hat. Nobody else seemed to suspect a thing. Even Knox was laughing and jumping up and down with excitement. Only Piers didn't join in.

Everyone carried on begging Esme to do the trick again as the bell rang and we headed back to the classroom.

"Settle down, Indigo Class. It is time for our afternoon lessons," said Miss Marker firmly. "Take your hat off please, Esme. You can put it back on at going-home time."

As Esme slid the top hat out of sight underneath our table, Miss Marker turned to the whiteboard. This time it was covered with sums.

$$24 \div 2 = 12$$
$$6 \times 3 = 18$$
$$19 - 4 = 15$$

"I hope you've all been practising your times tables in the holidays," she said. "Have a go at these multiplication questions."

The class groaned. But I was pleased – I recognized this type of sum. Back in the Magic Realm, we always used ingredients for spells and potions to help us work out the answers:

1 jar of eyeballs
x 1 jar of eyeballs
= 1 jar of eyeballs

2 newt tongues
x 2 newt tongues
= 4 newt tongues

3 slippery snake skins
x 3 slippery snake skins
= 9 slippery snake skins

I shuddered as I remembered the horrible wallchart with pictures of pickled brains that used to hang on the wall of the Toadstool Spell Group. It was supposed to help us with our six times table. (The seven times table was skeleton fingers. And eight was rats' tails.) But what should I count with today, I wondered, trying to think of something much nicer. After the magic I did this morning, rabbits came hopping into my mind straight away, of course.

I glanced at the first question.

$$1 \times 10 =$$

"Easy," I mumbled, waving my fluffy pen, ready to write the answer. "Take one rabbit and times by ten... You will have ten rabbits then!"

I glanced at the next question.

$$9 \times 10 =$$

"Goodness!" I giggled to myself. "This sum has lots of bunnies now... Nine times ten is ... ninety. Wow!"

I was about to write down the answer when I heard Esme let out a tiny gasp.

"Look, Bella!" she whispered. "Down there!"

I peeped under the table. The gold hat was wobbling from side to side.

A pair of long fluffy ears appeared, and then a pink twitching nose, and a small smoky-grey rabbit popped his head up.

"That's not Nibbles," I gulped.

"No," agreed Esme under her breath. "And nor is that."

A chocolate brown one had appeared now too ... then a speckled one ... and a shy black one with a quivering nose.

"Where are they coming from?" I gawped.

"This really is multiplication," Esme giggled.

Multiplication – of course! Suddenly I knew what had happened. These were the magic rabbits I had imagined just now as I muttered my sum and waved my pen . . . except it wasn't just a pen, of course. It was also a magic wand.

"Five!" whispered Esme excitedly. "Look!" She pointed to a floppy-eared golden rabbit jostling inside the hat too.

"Six," I groaned as a snowy-white one squeezed in.

"Is something the matter, girls?" asked Miss Marker, looking up from her desk.

I shook my head, hoping Esme wasn't going to say anything either. The children in Indigo Class might believe one rabbit was a simple magician's trick, but not a whole hatful. How were we going to explain that?

Chapter Six

Esme and I peeped under the table again. The magic hat was still wobbling as the six little bunnies looked over the top.

"Seven!" squealed Esme as a pair of long ginger ears appeared too. "Sorry, miss. I was just counting out loud," she said quickly.

I shot her a grateful smile. My hands were shaking. I had no idea what to do. Out of the corner of my eye, I saw the little speckled bunny and the smoky-grey one tumble out of the hat. The chocolate-brown one followed.

"Get back in that hat right now, please!" I clicked my teeth and squeaked at them under my breath in their own Rabbit language. If I didn't put a stop to this soon, there'd be bunnies hopping all over the classroom.

I glanced at the first sum I had written: $1 \times 10 = 10$. There were seven bunnies in the hat already. I had a horrible feeling there would be three more before this spell was done.

Sure enough, a pair of very fluffy-looking ears appeared. "Tumbling toadstools!" I yelped. "That makes eight!"

"I beg your pardon, Bella?" said Miss Marker.

"Er. . ." I stammered as Zac glanced under the table too. As soon as he spotted the rabbits, he nudged Zoe and their dark eyes grew as big as cauldron lids.

"Er. . ." I stammered again, fiddling with my pink flamingo pen. If only I could wave it in the air and disappear the rabbits before the whole class noticed.

"Are you all right, Bella? You look a little anxious. . ." Miss Marker stood up and walked towards me.

"Er. . ." My mind was whirring like a windmill. The rabbits had hopped back inside the hat. But I knew they wouldn't stay there long. They were far too fidgety.

Esme suddenly leant forward and felt my brow. "I don't think Bella feels very well, miss. She looks like she's going to be sick!" she said.

"Eww!" squealed Malinda and Fay.

"I think she ought to get to the toilet!" said Esme. "She ate an awful lot of sprouts at lunchtime..."

"That's it! The sprouts," I said, understanding Esme's brilliant plan. If I could leave the classroom, perhaps there was a way I could take the rabbits with me. "I really don't feel well," I said, making a horrible gulping noise like a lizard swallowing a fly.

"Use my hat! Just in case you don't make it..." said Esme, leaping to her feet.

"Eww!" screamed just about everybody in the whole class. Even Miss Marker took a step backwards.

"Don't worry. I'll take her," said Esme, putting her arm around me with a totally straight face. She should be on telly-vision she can act so well.

The twins were looking worried too, although they must have guessed this was all just a way to hide the rabbits.

I'm not nearly so good at acting, but I

51

tried my best to look sick as I hunched over the hat.

"Keep down and don't let your ears show!" I whispered, clicking my teeth at the tiny rabbits in their own language. Then Esme and I ran out of the door as fast as we could.

"Steady. Where are you two off to?" said our head teacher as we nearly bumped into him coming round the corner.

"Er. . ." I gulped.

"Breath of fresh air. Bella doesn't feel well," said Esme, flinging open the doors to the playground.

I counted the rabbits again as we ran outside. Still only eight. Perhaps the spell had stopped after all.

"If they squeeze under the gate, they can follow Nibbles to the village green," said Esme.

"Good idea!" I agreed as the bunnies tumbled out of the hat and hopped away. I wished we could keep them somehow. But, just like Nibbles, they seemed happier in the wild.

"Look," cried Esme. "They've got magic stars too."

She was right. Even though the bunnies were all different, each one had a star shape right in the middle of its tail.

"Let's call that one Smoky," said Esme as the grey rabbit disappeared along the lane. The shy black rabbit darted after him. The star on her tail was bright white.

"That one should be Midnight," said Esme.

"Goodbye, Chocolate!" I joined in as the dark-brown rabbit scurried off. "And Ginger. And Snowy... And Speckles too."

"And Fluffy!" we both cried as the soft,

long-haired rabbit hopped away.

"And goodbye, Bunnykins the Second," Esme laughed as the little yellow rabbit with the very long ears followed after them all. "He's my favourite," she said. "He looks just like my baby brother's stuffed toy."

"See if you can find Nibbles. He must be somewhere nearby," I called, clicking my teeth and talking to the rabbits in their own language.

"It's so cool you can do that!" said Esme. She clicked her teeth too. Unfortunately, she said something VERY rude. The rabbits turned and glared at her.

"Whoops! I'd better leave the talking to you." Esme blushed. She bent down to pick up the hat. "Look! There's another one," she cried as a little black-and-white bunny yawned and popped his head over the top. "Another two!" She laughed as a similar one

54

with brown-and-white patches followed.

"Leaping leprechauns! I knew there'd be more!" I groaned.

The two new rabbits blinked sleepily as if they had been having a lovely nap when a spell whisked them away.

"Cosy and Dozy!" Esme smiled, lifting the sleepy rabbits out of the hat. "That makes ten altogether," she said as they hopped off.

"Eleven if you count Nibbles!" I reminded her.

Esme turned the hat upside down and shook it. No more rabbits came tumbling out.

"That's all of them now," I said, with a sigh of relief. At least I never finished writing my second sum. "Eleven magic rabbits is quite enough!"

Chapter Seven

As soon as school was over, Esme and I ran outside.

"Hello, Bella!" A smile spread across Aunty Rose's round apple cheeks. "How was your very first day at school?"

"Wonderful!" I said, giving her a big hug. "But will it be all right if I go home with Esme to work on our Roman homework together?"

"Of course!" said Aunty Rose. "I'll ask

Uncle Martin to pick you up from the windmill at seven."

"Thank you! I'll tell you all about being in Indigo Class later," I called as Esme grabbed my hand and we dashed away to catch the bus.

"Are you sure you don't mind that I'm a top-secret witch?" I whispered to her as we rattled along the country lanes.

"Mind? I think it's MAGICAL!" said Esme, bouncing up and down on the seat. "We're going to have so much fun together. Especially if. . ."

I glanced over and saw that she was blushing.

"Especially if we can be best friends," she said.

"Best friends?" I couldn't believe it! "Jumping jellyfish! I'd love that!" I said. I thought Esme might want to throw me in

58

gaol or boil me in a pot when she found out I was a witch. Instead, we were best friends already.

The only real friend I'd had back in the Magic Realm was Gawpaw the troll. Gawpaw's idea of fun wasn't always quite the same as mine...

But as Esme chattered excitedly about tea and cake and doing our homework together, I knew that I had met the best Person friend I could ever wish for.

"There's just one thing," she said, suddenly looking worried. "Don't expect the windmill to be smart. It's old and draughty and..."

"Beautiful!" I smiled as the tall white

building came into view. I had seen the windmill before of course, when I'd flown here secretly on a dark night to try and find Rascal's mother. But now the sun was shining and I could see the white sails rattling in the breeze and the bright-blue window sills looking out over an apple orchard and a grassy meadow. "It's lovely!" I said.

"I knew you'd like it! Piers says it's a dump, but he's wrong!" cried Esme, jumping down from the bus as it stopped.

"Mum, this is Bella," she called to a woman with wild red hair who seemed to be scribbling notes in a little book as she waved to us from the side of the lane. "We are best friends and we're going to do our homework together. Can she stay for tea?"

"Of course!" Mrs Lee peered over her lopsided spectacles and smiled at me kindly.

"Welcome to our windmill, Bella. It's not much, but it's home."

"We had to come here when Piers's dad threw us out of our flat in the village," explained Esme as we made our way across the meadow. "He closed down Mum's bookshop too, just because we were one day late with the rent."

"He wanted to turn the whole building into fancy new offices for his company, Seymour Cement. They make concrete," sighed Mrs Lee.

"That's terrible," I said.

But Esme shook her head. "He was trying to bully us, but it didn't work. This old windmill used to belong to my great-grandfather and we love it here."

"I know what you mean," I smiled. It was supposed to be a punishment when Aunt Hemlock sent me to live in the Person World. But it was the best thing that had ever happened to me.

"Now Mum's not running the bookshop, she has enough time to try to write her own stories. That's why she's in a dream half the time!" Esme giggled as Mrs Lee stopped in the middle of the meadow to scribble in her notebook. "She's always trying to think up new ideas. But we don't mind. Me and Gretel can pick blackberries and play outside in the meadow. And Jack the Bean can nap in the sun." She pointed to a pram parked in the shade of an apple tree where her baby brother was sleeping. Little Gretel was skipping in and out of a row of bright-orange pumpkins.

"No matter what Piers says, the Seymours can't bully us any more. I'm not scared of them. Not one little bit," said Esme, doing a cartwheel across the grass.

"Oh no!" she cried suddenly, touching the top of her head as she landed in a heap under an apple tree. "I left my top hat by the bus stop on the village green."

"What's that?" said Mrs Lee, looking up

from her notebook. "Who's on the village green?"

"Not who," giggled Esme. "What! I left my hat behind."

"I'm sure it will still be there in the morning," smiled Mrs Lee.

I thought about the eleven magic rabbits that would be out on the village green tonight too.

"I hope Nibbles and his friends will be all right," I whispered.

Chapter Eight

Esme's attic bedroom was at the very top of the windmill. It was a terrible mess with books and clothes and comics all over the floor.

"Sorry!" she blushed, clearing a space so we could flop down on her bed.

I didn't mind a bit. The room seemed just like Esme herself – bursting and bubbling over with fun. There was even a long stripy sock hanging from the lampshade.

"What about your dad?" I asked as Esme pulled a patchwork quilt over our knees. "Does he like living at the windmill too?"

A shadow flickered over Esme face. "Dad doesn't live with us any more," she said. "He and Mum separated last year, just before Jack the Bean was born."

"Oh," I said, wishing that I had never asked her. "You must miss him a lot."

"That's why I wanted to get good at magic," Esme sighed. "He used to do conjuring tricks too. Not that they ever worked. Mum says the only trick he was ever any good at was disappearing!"

Esme laughed as if she had made a joke, but she didn't look happy. "My parents disappeared too," I told her. "That's why Aunt Hemlock had to look after me. They turned themselves into white mice. But with so many witches' cats in the Magic Realm, something terrible must have happened. All that was ever found were two pink tails."

"That's awful!" gasped Esme. "Can't you do a spell to try and bring them back?" I saw a leap of hope in her eyes. "Perhaps you could make my dad come home too?"

I shook my head. It was difficult to explain. "Magic doesn't work like that. Witches can't just undo horrid things and change them back again," I said.

I expected Esme to look disappointed, but a little smile crept over her face. "Could you do some real magic now, though? I mean just a *tiny* spell. A *teeny-tiny* one, just to show me how it works?" she begged.

I knew I shouldn't...

But I thought how sad Esme must be about her dad. If there was any way that I could cheer her up ... even a little bit.

"Just one *teeny-tiny* spell," I said, glancing

round the room to see what I could do.

My eyes came to rest on the long stripy sock, hanging from the lampshade. "Perfect!"

I held out my wand.

Stripy sock hanging there,
Dance around and . . .
Er . . .
. . . and find your pair!

Wheee! A rainbow of sparkly light shot from the end of my wand.

"Cool!" cheered Esme.

I had to admit it was pretty amazing. The straggly sock came to life, as if an invisible foot was dancing inside it. It spun and kicked and twirled in the air, even turning upside down to do a little tap dance on the ceiling. Then it shot across the floor and suddenly there were two of them – two long stripy socks dipping and bowing as if they were a man and a woman on the  ballroom-dancing programme Aunty Rose likes to watch on telly-vision.

Slowly, they rolled themselves into a ball and came to rest beside Esme's overflowing laundry basket.

"Wow!" she said. "That was amazing! I don't suppose... I mean, could we..."

"Magically tidy up your room?" I grinned. I just had exactly the same idea.

I leapt to my feet, bouncing on the bed as I waved my wand three times in the air.

Magic spell, do what you can,
Make this room spick and span!

Boom! It was as if an earthquake had struck.

Shelves shook. The bed wobbled. A chair toppled over.

Then a whirlwind of comics, books, shoes and clothes swirled around us.

"Duck!" cried Esme, and we buried our heads under the patchwork quilt.

"Sorry! I think I've overdone it again," I gasped.

But Esme peeped out from under the corner of the blanket. "No," she said. "Look!"

I lifted my head. The storm was over. Esme's room was as neat and perfect as the Sellwell Department Store. All the books were on the bookshelves. All the clothes were on hangers. Even her little doll's house was tidy.

"Whomping wizards!" I gasped.

71

"Whomping wizards indeed! I don't think it's *ever* looked as neat as this," gulped Esme.

Suddenly, the door swung open. The sound of a howling baby filled the room.

"What's going on in here girls? You've woken Jack the Bean," said Mrs Lee, jiggling the red-faced baby. "I was trying to do some writing. I thought the whole windmill was going to fall down."

"Sorry, Mum. We were just tidying up," said Esme calmly.

Mrs Lee's mouth fell open as she stepped properly into the room and looked around. "Well I never, Esmeralda Tinkerbell Lee! I don't think your bedroom has ever been so tidy. Thank you, Bella. You must be a very good influence."

"I can't believe she told you my middle name is Tinkerbell," groaned Esme as Mrs Lee went back down the stairs.

"Don't worry, mine is Bat-Ears!" I confessed.

Esme snorted with laughter. Then she spun me around the room. "Well, Belladonna Bat-Ears, thank you!" she said. "It was lovely to see Mum looking happy. She's been so worried about everything since Dad left and we lost the bookshop. . ."

"No! Thank you," I said, sinking into a dizzy heap on the tidy floor "That's the first time anyone has ever asked me to do magic just for fun. It felt. . ." How could I describe it?

"Amazing?" asked Esme.

"Sparkly!" I said. My fingers were still tingling as I held my wand.

Chapter Nine

Esme stood in the middle of her tidy bedroom holding out our green Merrymeet School book bags.

"Please, Bella!" she begged.

"No! We can't use magic to do our homework," I gasped.

"I don't see why not." Esme smiled at me with her big blue eyes. "Think how furious Piers and the Mars gang would be if everyone on Mercury table got a gold star for their Roman homework. The twins are so clever that theirs will be brilliant anyway. And if we use a little magic..."

"Wouldn't that be cheating?" I said. "I know we just tidied your room with a spell, but it's not the same. Isn't homework meant to help Persons learn things?"

"Humph! I thought witches were supposed to be wicked. But I suppose you're right," sighed Esme. "Come on! We'd better go downstairs and use the computer instead."

"Computers are like Person magic. I think they are brilliant," I said as we sat at the kitchen table.

"Oh dear! I don't think Mum's had a very good day," said Esme, pointing to six empty coffee cups and a pad of paper beside the computer. Mrs Lee had obviously been trying to write her book. But she seemed a little stuck.

A Story About ... (Something?)
by Pandora Lee

Once upon a time there was a ... ?

After that there was just a lot of crossing out and scribbling.

"At least she's made a start," I said, thinking how difficult it had been to write about my summer holidays. "And I always love a story that begins *Once upon a time. . .*"

"Me too!" said Esme, typing on the computer. A new screen appeared.

"We have to find out one really interesting thing," she reminded me. I peered over her shoulder as we read all about the Romans building straight roads and inventing the calendar. But we had already learnt about those things with Miss Marker in school.

We looked further down the page.

"Look!" we cried at exactly the same time.

It is believed that the Romans introduced the first rabbits to Ancient Britain.

"Perfect!" said Esme, spreading out a big sheet of paper. "I'll do the writing if you do one of your brilliant pictures. Just don't make the rabbit look anything like Nibbles or Piers will be furious!"

Suddenly there was a terrible sound — as if a hundred rattling suits of armour were stomping around the windmill. "Scampering scorpions! What's that noise?" I gasped, nearly jumping out of my skin.

"It's just our funny old telephone," said Esme, leaping to her feet to answer it. "Hello?" As she listened to the voice on the other end of the big red receiver, her face turned white as a ghost.

"Yes, Mr Seymour... Yes. I understand," she said slowly. "I'd better call Mum."

She covered the phone with her shaking hand.

"It's Piers's dad," she whispered. "He says we have one week to move out of the windmill. He says he's going to bulldoze it to the ground..."

Chapter Ten

Mrs Lee poured us all a cup of tea as she explained everything Mr Seymour had threatened to do.

"We must try and keep calm. Perhaps we can appeal to the council," she said. But, as she lifted the pot, I saw her hands were shaking. "He says he is going to knock down the windmill, bulldoze the meadow and build a concrete car park here instead."

"He can't do that!" Esme gasped. "He

doesn't even own the windmill. It's been in our family for generations."

"I'm afraid he can," said Mrs Lee, sadly. "He's sending over some documents to prove it, but . . . well, it seems my grandfather owed money to Mr Seymour's grandfather. . ."

"So he sold him the windmill," groaned Esme.

"The worst thing is, the Seymours didn't even want it," said Mrs Lee, shaking her head. "They just left it empty to rot."

"But it's so beautiful here. . . And it's your home. Surely Persons can't just go around knocking down windmills whenever they feel like it?" I cried.

"I am afraid Mr Seymour is a very powerful man. If the paperwork is right, he can do what he likes," said Mrs Lee. "He claims he needs somewhere to park his lorries. The ones that deliver concrete up and down the country. He is in a terrible rush about it all of a sudden. . ."

"This is because of Piers!" Esme swallowed hard. I could see she was trying not to cry. "He. . . Well, something happened to him at school today, Mum. Everyone laughed . . . and he thought it was my fault."

"It wasn't Esme's fault," I said. "It was mine." If only I hadn't interfered with her trick. Then Nibbles would never have appeared inside her hat . . . and he would never have bitten Piers's nose. I was right. Magic *always* causes trouble in the Person World.

"It was Piers's own fault. He was being horrible as usual," said Esme. "But when everyone laughed, he promised to get revenge on me."

"And now the Seymours are going to turn us out of our home. It's like the bookshop all over again," sighed Mrs Lee.

"We were just getting settled in," said Esme. "I know there's still so much to do. But I painted the windows and Gretel planted flowers. . ."

"That's what's so sad," agreed Mrs Lee. "It really did feel as if the old place was magically coming back to life."

"*Magically*?" whispered Esme, grabbing my arm. "That's it! There *is* something we can do. Why didn't I think of it before? Come on, Bella."

She pulled me towards the door.

"Don't worry, Mum. I've got a plan," she beamed. "I mean, not yet. But Bella's going to help. And we'll save the windmill, I promise. Just you wait and see. . ."

Esme sat me down under an apple tree in the meadow.

It was dark. Uncle Martin would be here to pick me up soon. I could see Mrs Lee talking to Gretel in the warm orange light of the kitchen. Even from far away I could tell the little girl was crying and stamping her feet as she heard how the windmill would be knocked down.

"Please help us," said Esme. "You're a witch. There must be something you can do?"

"You mean with magic?" I asked. My heart was pounding. Until I reached the Person World, I couldn't even turn a shoelace into a worm. Now Esme was asking me to save her family home.

"Yes!" she cried. "Surely you can use a spell to stop Mr Seymour's plan?"

"Clattering cauldrons! Maybe I can!" I leapt to my feet and grasped my wand. It felt brilliant to have someone believe in my magic skills at last. "What sort of spell do you want?"

"I don't know *exactly*. . ." Esme paced up and down in the gloom.

There had to be something. But what sort of spell could possibly stop Mr Seymour?

"Got it!" cried Esme. "You need to turn back time and make him change his mind!"

I froze on the spot. "I can't do that," I said. "No witch can."

I wish I had listened more in the Magical Methods lessons we used to have back in the Toadstool Spell Group. But I knew for sure there are three things no witch or wizard can ever do:

THE BIG THREE RULES.

1. Magic cannot be used to make money or gold. (If it could, Aunt Hemlock would have filled her cave with coins.)

2. Magic cannot undo death. (If only it could! I would have spent every day trying to bring my parents back to life.)

3. Magic cannot change the course of time. (If it could, I would have travelled back to that same moment I lost Mum and Dad, and told them never to turn themselves into white mice.)

"I'm sorry, Esme. It's just not possible," I said. "But you're right. There has to be something I can do. Some sort of spell."

I paced up and down again. Thinking... Desperately thinking.

"It doesn't matter," said Esme at last. It was so dark now I couldn't see her face, but I knew what she must be feeling. *Why can't magic be used for something useful?*

Not like dancing socks. But for real things — things that really matter. And she was right.

If I couldn't bring my own parents back, or make Esme's dad come home, or save the windmill, then what was the point?

Nothing! Magic was useless.

Chapter Eleven

I barely slept at all that night. Rascal, my little kitten, was snoring on the end of my bed. But I kept tossing and turning. I couldn't think of any spell or magic potion that could stop Mr Seymour knocking the windmill to the ground.

"What shall I do?" I said in Cat Chat, burying my head in Rascal's soft grey fur. "I feel like I've let Esme down."

"Shh!" He batted me away with a

fluffy grey paw. "I'm dreaming I'm a lion in Africa." Moments later he was snoring again.

"More like a rhinoceros than a lion," I whispered, getting up and going to look out of the window.

All I could see in the moonlight was the big dark shape of Hawk Hall: the Seymours' huge, horrible grey house that sits right next door to our little cottage. There isn't a single flower in their garden. Not even a blade of grass. Just three shiny grey cars parked on the grey driveway and grey concrete all around.

"Horrible!" I shuddered. No wonder the Seymours didn't care what happened to the windmill or the ancient orchard and the meadow. They didn't seem to know anything about nature or beauty...

There was a flash of movement in our

garden and by the light of a street lamp I saw a fluffy white tail with a star on it disappearing under the hedge. "Speckles!" I cried, recognizing one of the magic rabbits from yesterday. I opened the window and clicked my teeth in Rabbit language. But she had already hurried away. She wasn't heading towards Hawk Hall, of course, as there was nothing on all that concrete for a little rabbit to eat.

I was still yawning when Uncle Martin and Aunty Rose walked me to school the next morning.

"I hope you have something nice for lunch today," said Aunty Rose.

"Steer clear of the sprouts!" chuckled Uncle Martin.

"I will," I agreed. But I was finding it hard to concentrate as I thought I saw

Speckles disappearing behind a parked car.

By the time we reached the village green, I had seen Bunnykins the Second lolloping along the footpath. Cosy and Dozy were fast asleep on the doormat outside the pub. And I thought I saw Smoky in a garden behind the post office.

I didn't point the bunnies out to Aunt Rose and Uncle Martin in case they asked too many questions about where they had come from. But I was glad to see the magic bunnies all the same. They had hurried away from school so fast yesterday that I hadn't really had time to think about where they would live. But it was lovely to imagine them happily making their homes all around Merrymeet.

"What's all this then?" said Uncle Martin, pointing to a large crowd of grown-up Persons who seemed to have gathered in front of the school. Some of them were still wearing their pyjamas.

"They don't look very happy," he said.

"Oooh!" said Aunty Rose. "Maybe they've heard about Mr Seymour's terrible plan to turn Mrs Lee and those poor kiddies out of their home and cover that beautiful meadow with concrete! News travels fast in Merrymeet."

But, as we drew closer, it quickly became clear it wasn't the windmill the crowd was worried about.

I caught snatches of conversation: "Whiskers..." "Lop-ears..." "Long-ears..." "Cottontails..." "Burrow-diggers..."

But one word kept being repeated over and over again.

"RABBITS!"

"Rabbits?" said Aunty Rose in surprise.

"They've eaten all my parsley!" said old Mrs Brimblecombe from the post office.

"And dug holes all over the churchyard," said the vicar.

"And eaten nearly everything in the allotments!" thundered a tall woman in green wellingtons. "We have the Harvest Festival Gardening Competition coming up! If this carries on, we're doomed."

"That's Lady Trim — she's head of the council," whispered Uncle Martin.

"There are swarms of rabbits chomping our cabbages!" said a man with a rake.

"A plague of bouncing bunnies!" agreed Lady Trim.

Swarms? A plague? What were they talking about? Surely eleven little bunnies couldn't cause all this trouble...

Just then I saw Esme running towards me from the bus stop. She was waving her gold top hat wildly in the air, pointing to something behind me.

"Look!" she cried.

I turned around and saw the village green for the first time...

The whole area was covered — absolutely smothered — with rabbits. Big ones. Small ones. Brown ones. White ones. Ginger ones. Grey ones. All different ... except each one had a perfect magic star on its tail!

"Popping potions! They must have appeared in the hat during the night," I whispered, remembering how Esme had left it at the village bus stop by mistake.

"Multiplication!" hissed Esme, dragging me to one side. "I thought you only did one magic sum yesterday?"

"Oh dear..." I had a horrible squirmy feeling in my tummy as I remembered the second multiplication sum I had begun:

$$9 \times 10 =$$

"Ninety!" I thought. I had never actually written down the answer, but chanting the sum and accidentally waving the magic pen in my hand must have been enough. "I will never use my flamingo biro for doing maths ever again!" I groaned. "There are ninety new rabbits now, plus the ten from yesterday. That makes. . ."

"One hundred!" said Esme.

"One hundred and one!" I said as I spotted Nibbles greedily chewing the corner of a little boy's lunch box.

Lady Trim clapped her hands loudly.

"We can't have rabbits rampaging all over the village," she announced. "They'll eat everything in our gardens."

A large silver car pulled up at the edge of the green and Mr Seymour climbed out. Everyone fell silent.

"This is all Esme Lee's fault," he said, pointing at her as Piers climbed out of the car too. "My boy here says she was doing stupid magic tricks all day yesterday. She made a rabbit appear in a hat."

"A vicious one," said Piers, rubbing his nose.

I thought I heard old Mrs Brimblecombe from the post office giggle. But everybody else was staring at Esme.

"It's not her fault!" I said quickly.

"Do you know anything about this, Esme?" asked our head teacher.

"It's true. I was practising conjuring," said Esme. "Then Nibbles appeared. He's the bunny who bit Piers on the nose..."

"Gracious me!" Now old Mrs Brimblecombe really was giggling.

"Ladies and gentlemen," the head teacher raised his voice, "I must ask you to move away from school so that we can take the children inside and begin our lessons. I was aware there was some fun with conjuring tricks going on in the playground yesterday, but I am sure none of you are seriously suggesting that a little girl can be responsible for all these rabbits."

"I don't care who is responsible!" said Lady Trim. "We are going to have to put a stop to these greedy pests before they eat every vegetable in Merrymeet!"

"Leave it to me!" said Mr Seymour, climbing back into his shiny grey car. "I'll have this village rid of rabbits by tomorrow morning. Just you wait and see. . ."

Chapter Twelve

"Oh, Esme. What are we going to do?" I said as soon as we were safely inside our classroom.

"About the bunnies?" she whispered.

"Yes. And the windmill," I groaned. Everything that had gone wrong was all because of my magic.

"Well, we've still got a week until the bulldozers arrive in the meadow," said Esme. "That gives us time to think of something to save the windmill. But Mr Seymour said he was going to get rid of the rabbits tomorrow."

"So bunnies first?" I said.

"Bunnies first!" agreed Esme.

"I don't know what Mr Seymour is planning, but it will be something horrible!" I shivered. "We need to find the bunnies somewhere new to live ... and quickly."

"They definitely can't stay in the village," agreed Esme. "Nobody wants a plague of rabbits eating their vegetables and digging up their gardens. Especially Lady Trim and the Allotment Committee. They win the Harvest Festival Gardening Competition every year. They won't risk ruining their chance of that."

"But where can we find a new home for so many rabbits?" I said. "They'll need plenty of space and lots of grass to eat."

"Windmill Meadow would be perfect," whispered Esme as Miss Marker began taking the register. "But that's no good now Mr Seymour is going to cover it with concrete!" She chewed her lip. "Operation Rabbit Rescue will meet again at break."

I gave a quick thumbs up.

"Who'd want to be a conjurer," she whispered, her eyes sparkling, "when they could be an undercover agent working to free rabbits from an evil villain instead?"

That was the brilliant thing about Esme. She always kept smiling. If she was disappointed I hadn't come up with a magic spell to save the windmill, she didn't show it.

"So," said Miss Marker brightly. "Who found out some interesting facts about the Romans?"

I hesitated. Our project looked amazing – Uncle Martin had helped me burn the edges and I'd dipped it in tea to make it look like a brilliant ancient scroll. But Esme and I looked at each other and we both shook our heads. This really wasn't the right moment to announce that the Romans had introduced rabbits to Ancient Britain. Any talk of bunnies would just make everyone more suspicious that the fluffy-tailed invasion of Merrymeet was all Esme's fault.

Luckily, Piers's hand shot up in the air. "Did you know, miss, it was the Romans who invented CONCRETE!"

The whole class groaned.

"Quiet please! That is very interesting!" said Miss Marker. And she listened to some of the different things the class had found out. When she came back to Mercury table again, the twins had so much to say about Roman shopping that she didn't seem to notice Esme and I had missed our turn. I slipped the scroll into my bag.

"Well done, everyone!" she said at last. "You have all worked very hard. We are going to have a wonderful time with our Roman project. And, to make it even more special, we are going on a trip tomorrow."

"A trip?" Everybody clapped their hands and cheered.

"We are going to the ruins of a Roman villa about an hour up the road," said Miss Marker. "The coach will arrive first thing and we can take packed lunches and stay all day. I hope we can have a picnic outside. The villa is part of an old Roman farm so there are acres and acres of grassland with beautiful fields and woods..."

"Boring! Who cares about fields," muttered Piers under his breath. "Will there be any swords and spears, miss?"

But Esme and I were practically jumping out of our seats with excitement – we'd both had the exact same thought.

"Fields!" I whispered, as Miss Marker explained about some of the things we could see in the visitors' centre.

"Fields full of *grass*," mouthed Esme.

"And woods too!" I squeezed her hand. "Are you thinking what I am thinking?"

Esme nodded. "Operation Rabbit Rescue has just found our long-eared friends a new home."

"Perfect!" I grinned. "All we've got to do now is get one hundred and one rabbits to come along on our school trip."

Chapter Thirteen

It was hard for Esme and I to talk much for the rest of the day. The twins wanted to play with us at break time. Then we had a noisy music lesson in the big hall. Everybody in Indigo Class was given a recorder. We were supposed to play a tune called "Twinkle, Twinkle, Little Star". But none of us were very good. It sounded more like "Screechy, Screechy, Squawky Crow".

"Oh dear," sighed Miss Marker. "I think

you had better put your recorders away in your book bags and practise a little at home."

At last it was lunchtime. (No more sprouts for me – I had pizza. Delicious!) Then Esme and I sat outside on the Friendship Bench where people can go for a quiet chat. We huddled together, trying to come up with the perfect plan to sneak the rabbits on to the school coach.

"I'll get up really early in the morning, go to the village green, and call all the rabbits together," I said. "I'll tell them they're in danger if they stay here, but they will be safe at the Roman villa. And then—"

"What are you two whispering about?" asked Piers, appearing behind us like a shadow. "I know you're up to something. . ."

We just smiled and skipped off to the other side of the playground.

"Look! There's Nibbles now," said Esme,

pointing through the railings as the fat little bunny hopped over the zebra crossing outside school. "You can tell him what's happening. Thank goodness you can talk to animals. You're so clever, Bella!"

"Psst!" I said, feeling proud as I pressed my face against the railings and twitched my nose. "I need to talk to you," I said, calling out to Nibbles in rabbit language.

"Not now!" He chomped his teeth as he spotted a juicy-looking dandelion leaf on the the side of the lane. "Lunch!"

"Wait!" I called. But he hopped away.

This was impossible! Every time I tried to talk to Nibbles he was always thinking about his tummy.

"Rabbits may have long ears but they never seem to listen to me," I groaned.

"Looks like you're going to need help getting them together in the morning," said Esme.

"I know. But you'll be at the windmill," I sighed.

"Not if I stay at your house tonight," said Esme.

"You mean?"

"Exactly!" Esme grinned.

"Sleepover!" We both cheered.

Despite all the worry about the windmill and the rabbits, I felt as if a thousand happy frogs were hopping in my tummy.

"Aunty Rose won't mind one little bit!" I said.

"And I know Mum will agree to it, even though it's a school night. She wants to take my mind off everything that's happening at the windmill," said Esme.

"Of course." I squeezed her arm. "Don't worry. I'm going to make this the best sleepover ever," I promised. "It'll be magic!"

And it was.

Next morning, Esme and I were up at the crack of dawn. We gobbled down our breakfast and were ready to leave at least an hour before the coach was due to arrive for the school trip.

"Can we go out early?" I asked Uncle Martin as he handed us our packed lunches. "We want to see if all those rabbits are on the village green again."

"Fair enough," said Uncle Martin, who was often up early himself to go birdwatching. "As there's two of you, you can walk down by yourselves. Have a good time at the Roman villa."

"We will," I said as Esme grabbed her book bag and we hurried out of the door.

"Look!" I said as we passed the high iron gates of Hawk Hall.

A dark-grey van was parked on the drive. The back doors were open and we could see a terrible tangle of metal boxes inside with glinting rows of jagged spikes like dragon's teeth.

"Traps!" I gasped. "So that's what Mr Seymour's going to do. He's going to set traps for the rabbits," I had seen animal traps before. Aunt Hemlock used horrible sharp-jawed snares just like this.

"Bye bye, bunnies," grinned Mr Seymour, coming out of his house as an enormous man in a boiler suit closed the doors of the van.

"That's Knox's uncle, Bruiser Bailey," whispered Esme. "He works in security at Seymour Cement."

"Murmuring mountains!" I gulped. He was as big as a giant.

"Set those traps all around the village," said Mr Seymour as Bruiser Bailey climbed into the driver's seat. "If we can destroy those greedy little rabbits, everyone in Merrymeet will love me. Especially Lady Trim and her Allotment Committee. She's head of the council. If I save her precious garden she'll agree to anything I want. She'll let me knock down that old windmill and bulldoze the meadow without any trouble at all."

"I'll be pleased to see the back of the bunnies myself, sir," growled Bruiser in a voice like an ogre "I've got a little allotment of my own, you know."

"Just do the job, will you?" said Mr Seymour, turning back towards the house. "I don't see the point in flowers, or fruit, or lawns. Not when you can have a lovely patch like this. Isn't that right, son?"

Esme and I ducked as we saw Piers standing on the front steps admiring his concrete courtyard.

"I hate rabbits! Especially that Nibbles!" he said, still rubbing his nose.

"Tell you what, son," laughed Mr Seymour, "I'll get Bruiser to bring you back a fluffy bunny tail. You can wear it as a bow tie!"

"What a monster!" shivered Esme. But I grabbed her hand.

"Quick!" I hissed. "We've got to find the rabbits and tell them they're in terrible danger. Knox's uncle is going to start setting those traps right away."

Chapter Fourteen

Esme and I ran towards the village green.

"The sooner we get the rabbits safely to the Roman villa, the better," she puffed.

"We might be too late," I groaned as we dashed along the pavement past the allotments. A gaggle of furious-looking gardeners were marching up and down in wellington boots. There had been green rows of leaves yesterday. Now there was nothing but chewed-up stalks poking out of the mud.

"Those pesky rabbits have had my Brussels sprouts. I was saving them for Christmas dinner!" growled a red-faced man with a wheelbarrow.

"Yuck! Don't tell me rabbits like those things!" I whispered to Esme as we peeped over the hedge. I spotted Nibbles lolloping out from behind a watering can. His cheeks were bulging, with a Brussel sprout stuffed in each one.

"There's one of the little pests right now," cried Lady Trim, waving a spade. "Grab it by the ears!"

"Look out, Nibbles!" I squeaked.

Lady Trim's sharp spade missed his fluffy tail by a centimetre as he squeezed his fat bottom through a hole in the hedge.

"The sooner Mr Seymour sets those traps the better!" sighed Lady Trim as Nibbles lolloped off down the lane. "He's promised me a pair of rabbit-skin gardening gloves."

"How horrid!" I whispered as Esme and I crept away, keeping out of sight below the hedge. The whole village would be wearing rabbit fur if we didn't act fast.

"You really mustn't eat Persons' vegetables, Nibbles," I hissed as we turned the corner and caught up with him by a bridge over Merrymeet river.

The greedy little rabbit ignored me as usual and started to nibble the long, lush grass at the edge of the water.

"Look!" said Esme as her favourite rabbit, Bunnykins the Second, hopped into view.

He almost tripped over his long ears as he bumbled over the bridge towards us.

I spotted Cozy and Dozy, snoozing as usual, behind a log.

Then Speckles and Fluffy and Ginger scampered along the riverbank too.

"They're all here! The whole gang," I said, counting the group of eleven special magic bunnies we had given names to. Even shy Midnight poked her head out from under the bridge for a moment.

"Listen to me, bunnies! This is important," I said. To my amazement the rabbits turned towards me at last. Even Nibbles stopped chewing for a moment.

"You are in real danger!" Now I finally had their attention, I explained how Mr Seymour was planning to trap them. "Not just you, but every rabbit in the village," I said, thinking of the other ninety bunnies who must be close by somewhere.

"Tell them all to watch out for Knox's uncle," said Esme as I clicked my teeth together.

"He's as tough as a troll and big as a giant," I warned the rabbits. "And he drives a grey van. It's full of traps."

Dozy yawned. She reminded me of Rascal. "Shh! I'm too sleepy for all this," she said.

"Me too!" Cozy rolled into a ball.

"You're not listening to me!" I cried as the other bunnies started to hop away. I made a grab for Fluffy but was left with nothing but a handful of soft white hair. "Stop!"

Nibbles raised his head and sniffed the air. I held my breath – for a moment I thought he was going to call the other rabbits back. . .

Instead, he twitched his nose, hopped forward and chomped a mouthful of tall green reeds.

Behind us the church bells struck.

"We're running out of time," said Esme. "The coach will be here in half an hour."

"I don't know what to do," I groaned. The bunnies were setting off in all directions. They were absolutely adorable – especially these eleven that we had named – but they wouldn't listen to a word I said. "It's like I don't even speak their language."

"We'll have try something else," said Esme. "And quickly…"

We could hear the clanking rattle of the grey van coming up the lane.

"We need to think of a way to get the rabbits to follow us," I said.

"Like the Pied Piper!" Esme clapped her hands. "It's one of Mum's favourite fairy tales."

"The one with the rats?" I shuddered, remembering a horrible picture in Aunt Hemlock's storybook as the animals followed the Piper's tune.

"But we don't have any music," I sighed. Why was Esme talking about storybooks? We were wasting time. I glanced back to see Bruiser Bailey climbing out of the van to set a trap at the other end of the lane.

"We do have music," said Esme. "Look!" She rummaged in her book bag and pulled out her recorder. "Ta-da!"

"Spluttering serpents! You're brilliant!" I cried. "You be the Pied Piper and I'll add a little magic to the tune!"

Chapter Fifteen

As Esme danced across the bridge playing "Twinkle, Twinkle, Little Star" on her recorder, I waved my wand in the air.

Let us make a happy tune,
So the rabbits follow soon.
Little bunnies hop along,
As we play our merry song.

Instantly, Esme's squeaky recorder

sounded like a gentle flute.

"Wow!" she giggled, taking it out of her mouth for a moment. "I should audition for the school orchestra."

She blew again and I stepped backwards, watching in amazement as Nibbles turned and began following her over the bridge. It was as if the music was pulling him along on an invisible string. He hopped right past a clump of tall reeds without stopping to nibble them. By the time Esme reached the line of trees on the other side of the bridge, all eleven rabbits were following.

Even Cozy and Dozy sleepily joined the end of the line, hopping along as if they were still in a dream.

Dashing over the bridge behind them, I saw thirty or forty other rabbits all with the special magic stars on their tails. They were hopping towards us from every direction, following Esme's tune.

"Darting dragonflies, it's working!" I whooped.

Still piping, Esme danced a jig, kicking her heels high in the air as more and more rabbits joined the trail.

Luckily, it was so early in the morning that there was nobody on the village green. The road leading up to school was empty.

"Quick!" I yelped as I heard the rattle of Bruiser Bailey's van coming over the bridge behind us. "Hide!"

Esme dived behind a low stone wall. She

didn't even miss a note as the dancing rabbits followed her in a trance.

"Good morning, Mr Bailey," I called, hiding my fluffy wand-pen behind my back as the van came to a stop. Knox was sitting beside him in the front seat.

"Hello, Bella," Knox said as they both climbed out. He actually looked quite small beside his giant uncle. "Can you hear music?" he asked, scratching his head.

"Never mind that. We've got more important things to worry about!" growled Mr Bailey. "Have you seen any rabbits around here, young lady?"

"Rabbits? I don't think so..." I tried to sound surprised, as if he'd asked me about a herd of unicorns.

Bruiser Bailey shrugged his enormous shoulders. "Just tell me or this cloth-eared idiot here if you see so much as a whisker."

He grunted at Knox, who was standing with his head on one side as if he was still trying to work out where the sound of the recorder was coming from. It took all my effort not to glance towards the wall where I knew Esme and the band of bunnies were hiding.

"Get on with it then, lad," snapped Bruiser Bailey as Knox heaved a huge iron trap out from the back of the van and clattered to the side of the road. It had a swinging door and a horrible knot of chains and hooks, ready to catch any little creature who ventured inside.

"Oy, Cloth Ears, don't forget the carrot! You'll need bait," boomed Mr Bailey. "If we don't do this job properly Mr Seymour will put *us* in trap, never mind the bunny rabbits!"

"Sorry, Uncle Bruiser." Knox blushed so

red his face clashed with the juicy orange carrot he hung carefully inside the cage.

I saw Nibbles's pink nose pop out round the side of the wall. "Yum!" he said. His whiskers were poking out now too.

"Shoo!" I mumbled under my breath, waving my arms wildly behind Knox and Bruiser Bailey's backs. Trust Nibbles to be so greedy. He must have smelt the scent of carrot in the wind. One more sniff and he'd jump out right in front of us.

Behind the wall, the sound of Esme's recorder grew louder and faster. She must have spotted Nibbles trying to sneak away too.

Luckily Knox had climbed back inside the van. But Mr Bailey was scratching his head in exactly the same way his nephew had done.

"Do you know what? The boy's right.

I think I can hear music... Where can it be coming from?" he said, closing his eyes and nodding in time to the tune.

I only had a split second to act. Nibbles had come out from behind the wall and was standing on his hind legs. The moment Bruiser Bailey opened his eyes he would spot him for sure ... that's if Nibbles didn't just leap into the trap and sink his teeth into the juicy carrot right away.

Quick as the wind, I waved my wand and whispered under my breath:

Carrot in the metal box,
Turn into a smelly sock.

Pow!

There was a puff of yellow smoke and a terrible smell hit me right away. In place of the carrot was a long stringy sock – a bit like the one from Esme's bedroom, except this one was old and grey and very smelly. Nibbles's ears drooped with disappointment and he hopped back behind the wall.

"Poo!" Mr Bailey opened his eyes in surprise. "Never mind music. What's that horrible pong?"

"Er ... smells like cheese," I said.

"Cheese? We're trying to catch rabbits not mice!" Bruiser Bailey's mouth fell open as he stared at the trap. "Look what that idiot boy has done. I told him to hang a carrot and he's gone and put a sock in it instead."

Bruiser thumped on the roof of the van. "Get out here, Knox."

"I think a sock might work," I said quickly. "My aunt used to swear by them for catching goblins."

"Goblins?" Mr Bailey's eyes looked like

they were going to pop out of his head.

"I mean rabbits," I said quickly. (Though it is true, if ever you do want to catch a goblin, just hang up a really cheesy sock. The little creatures can't resist them.)

Knox staggered out of the van. A look of total surprise crossed his face as he saw the sock hanging in the trap. He opened his mouth to speak. Then, to my amazement, he nodded his head. "Rabbits do like socks," he said. "They use them to make nests, I think."

"Nests! I never heard such nonsense. They are rabbits not blinking birds!" said Mr Bailey, but he climbed back into the driver's seat and started the engine. "Come on, you great lummox. We haven't got time to muck about here."

"Don't worry, Bella – the trap wouldn't have worked anyway," whispered Knox mysteriously as he scrambled back into the van and it rumbled away down the lane.

As soon as the road was clear, Esme came out from behind the wall with hordes of hopping rabbits dancing around her in a ring. "Phew! That was a close one," she said. Even more rabbits seemed to have been drawn to the music and joined her while she was hiding.

"Find a partner and make a neat line, all of you," I ordered the bunnies, trying to count as quickly as I could. "Ninety-four, ninety-six, ninety-eight." It wasn't easy keeping track as they hopped about. "One hundred! One hundred and one! We've done it, Esme. Every single magic bunny is here!" I cried as they jostled behind Nibbles at the front of the line.

"Now all we need to do is get them on the coach..."

Chapter Sixteen

I took a turn at playing the enchanted recorder so that Esme could get her puff back. The rabbits hopped after me across the village green.

"Keep up, Bunnykins the Second," Esme laughed, running along beside us as her favourite bunny nearly fell over his ears again. She was right – he did look exactly like a real-life version of baby Bean's fluffy yellow toy.

It was funny to think that was where all the trouble had started ... with one stuffed rabbit and a magic hat. Now we had one hundred and one *real* rabbits to sneak out of Merrymeet without being spotted!

The coach was already parked beside the rubbish bins outside the school. Through the staffroom window, we could see the driver having a cup of coffee with Miss Marker.

"Quick," said Esme. "We need to get this lot on board before everybody starts to arrive."

"But how can we hide the rabbits?" I asked, suddenly realizing we hadn't thought the plan through. "They can't just sit on the seats like children."

"There's a storage space for suitcases underneath," said Esme, springing a latch on the side of the coach. "The bunnies can travel secretly in there."

"Brilliant!" I said, peering into the deep, dark space. But the rabbits backed away.

"I know it looks scary, but think of it like a cosy burrow," I said. "We're going to take you somewhere wonderful, I promise." I remembered the pictures of the lovely Roman villa. "You'll be safe and far away from Mr Seymour's traps. There'll be grass and woods and—"

"Brussels sprouts!" said Nibbles interrupting me.

"I'm not sure about that," I said. But Nibbles was already hopping out of line towards the bins. I blew the recorder, but Nibbles's nose was far stronger than the fading magic.

"It's the sprout peelings he's after!" cried Esme, pointing to a sack of green leaves beside the bins.

"Listen to me, bunnies!" I said, with a sharp blast on the recorder. "Everyone who hops into the coach can have a pile of lovely leaves all to themselves."

That did it! Quicker than any magic spell, Nibbles hopped into the suitcase space and a hundred hungry bunnies followed. Esme and I emptied the sack of sprout peelings in there with them and gently closed the hatch.

"You're going to love your new home," I whispered. Then Esme and I collapsed into each other's arms with relief.

"We did it!" she gasped. "Now all we'll need to do is secretly open the hatch when the coach is parked at the Roman villa and the rabbits will be free."

"I'll put another spell on the recorder,

so we can lead them somewhere safe when we arrive," I said.

"Good idea!" agreed Esme as I held the instrument in the air. I was just about to wave my wand when Miss Marker came out of the staffroom.

"I'll take that," she said, crossing the playground with the coach driver. "You won't need your recorder on the school trip." And she whisked it out of my hands.

"But..." began Esme.

"You won't want anything at all. Except maybe a pen to fill in a worksheet," said Miss Marker.

Esme looked panicked.

"Don't worry. As long as we are allowed a pen, I'll still have my magic wand," I whispered, tucking my pink flamingo biro safely behind my ear as the other children started to arrive.

The only school trip I had ever been on before was when the Toadstool Spell Group went to a fungus farm for the day. That time we all travelled in a flying cauldron and Nightshade Newtbreath, the class bully, sat on my head the whole way.

The coach trip was much more fun. Esme and I sat beside each other and the whole class sang songs. Esme knew all the words and taught me as we went along. The only time she fell quiet was when the coach reached the top of the hill and we passed the windmill.

I knew she was thinking about her family and what would happen when they were thrown out of their home.

"Oh look, it's my dad's new car park," Piers sniggered. "Won't it look lovely covered in concrete?" We could hear him from right at the back of the coach where he'd barged past everyone to get the best seat.

"He won't get away with it!" I said, squeezing Esme's hand. There were still six whole days until Mr Seymour brought his diggers in.

"I know," she whispered bravely. "If we can save one hundred and one bunnies, we can save one windmill. Right?"

"Right!" I agreed. Although I knew neither of us had any idea how to stop Mr Seymour's dreadful plan.

Somebody on the bus had started to sing a new song – perhaps because of all the bunnies they had seen scampering around the village yesterday.

Run, rabbit, run, rabbit –
Run! Run! Run!
Don't let the farmer have his fun!
Fun! Fun!

Everybody joined in at the top of their voices. Esme and I smiled at each other, thinking of the bunnies safely hidden away right beneath us in the bottom of the bus.

"Our rabbits aren't running – they're travelling in style!" giggled Esme.

"Just as long as the Roman villa is as green and grassy as it looked in the pictures," I said.

But we saw the rolling hills and thick woods long before we reached the entrance gates.

"This is perfect!" I whispered, leaping to my feet the minute the bus stopped. We were parked beside a thick hedgerow. "The bunnies can escape without anyone seeing them."

Esme and I slipped round the side of the coach while everybody else was still climbing down.

Esme flicked open the suitcase hatch and I poked my head inside. I could see hundreds of bright eyes shining at me in the darkness.

"I feel sick. I ate too many sprout leaves," groaned Nibbles.

"Hurry," said Esme. "Mrs Marker will be lining up the class."

"We'll leave the hatch open," I explained to the rabbits. "As soon as we've gone, hop out, follow the hedge and head for the woods. This place should make a perfect new home for you all."

"Esme? Bella? Where are you?" We heard Miss Marker calling us.

"Coming!" Esme grabbed my arm.

"Goodbye and good luck, bunnies!" I wished I could kiss each rabbit on the nose. I was going to miss them all ... especially greedy Nibbles, even though he was the most trouble. "Take care!" I whispered. We had brought them this far, but it was up to the rabbits to save themselves now.

Chapter Seventeen

The ruins of the Roman villa were really interesting. Even Miss Marker's worksheet was fun. We had to draw a picture of something we had seen. I copied the pattern of a beautiful mosaic floor.

I was so busy drawing, I nearly jumped out of my skin

when a real Roman Person tapped me on the shoulder.

"It's only an actor dressed up in a costume," laughed Esme, as I toppled over backwards in surprise.

The Actor Person led us all to a little Roman kitchen the museum had built. It had a real fire burning in the hearth and big clay pots. There was a pretend meal on the table and a jug of wine.

"Look, girls," said Miss Marker excitedly. "Do you see what the Roman family have caught for their dinner?"

Esme and I stared in horror. There was a bowl of clay birds' eggs and a rubbery fish on a plate. But hanging from the rafters was a rabbit.

"Don't worry. It's not real," said Miss Marker. "It's just a stuffed model made out of bits of old fur."

"Oh dear! When we found out about the Romans bringing rabbits to Ancient Britain, I didn't think about them *eating* them. I imagined they were pets." Esme gulped.

"Just as long as our magic bunnies don't see that," I whispered as we hurried away. "I don't want them thinking they are going to end up in a cooking pot!"

As I spoke, I thought I saw a flash of white – maybe Nibbles or Snowy – disappearing by the side of the ruins.

I dashed around the corner. But if it was one of the magic bunnies, it was already gone. "I hope they do as they're told and head to the safety of the woods as fast as they can," I said, looking across a patchwork of grassy fields to the thick line of trees.

"It's time for our lunch now!" called Miss Marker and we headed off to the picnic area.

Everyone was laughing and chatting

happily, when Malinda let out a furious cry. "Where's my cookie? Somebody must have eaten it." She scowled at poor Knox who was sitting beside her. "I bet it was you, wasn't it?"

"No!" said Knox. But he blushed so red I would have thought he was guilty too — if I hadn't spotted Nibbles for sure this time. He was hopping away under a picnic table with the giant cookie in his jaws.

"Naughty boy! Go to the woods with your friends," I hissed under my breath. He gave me a huffy look and waddled away with the biscuit clamped in his teeth.

I wondered if that really was the last we would see of the rabbits.

Esme and I kept glancing around all the

time another Roman Actor Person was showing us a display of weapons on the lawn. And I kept an extra-close lookout when we went to explore the Roman farm. But, at last, it seemed even Nibbles had done as he was told.

"I'll miss the rabbits, but the woods and fields really will make a perfect new home," I said as Esme and I ran ahead to be first back at the coach.

The door was open and the driver was dozing on the sunny grass. We tiptoed past him. The suitcase hatch was still ajar, just as we'd left it.

"It's empty," said Esme, poking her head right inside.

"Not even Cozy and Dozy having a nap?" I asked, just to be sure.

"All clear!" said Esme, checking one last

time before closing the latch.

Then we dashed around the side of the coach just as the rest of the class caught up.

Miss Marker took the register.

"Go right down to the back of the coach and fill up those seats first," she said to Esme and me, who were at the front of the line. Zac and Zoe joined us.

Piers looked furious. He had so much pocket money that he'd spent ages in the gift shop. Now he was the last one back to the coach. He was forced to sit right at the front beside Miss Marker. Fay and Malinda were opposite them, whispering about Knox being a biscuit thief.

"Can I sit there?" he asked, pointing at the last spare seat on the back row.

"Of course," I said, budging up so that Knox could stretch his long legs down the aisle. I smiled, wishing I could apologize that he was getting the blame for stealing Malinda's cookie when I knew it was really Nibbles all along.

Thinking of the greedy little rabbit, I stared out of the window to get one last view of the rolling fields.

"Look!" I whispered, leaning over Esme's shoulder as we both pressed our noses against the glass. We could see a smattering of little white dots made by the bunnies' tails as they hopped away towards the woods.

"Forty ... fifty ... sixty." I gave up trying to count. But they were all there, I was sure of it. "We did it!" I grinned. The bunnies were safe at last. Mr Seymour couldn't get them here.

The bus juddered down the bumpy driveway and joined the main road. Most of the class were already singing a funny song at the tops of their voices.

"Goodbye, bunnies," Esme and I whispered together as everyone else roared the noisy chorus.

And that's when I saw it... A little pink nose was twitching up at me, peeping out from underneath the seat in front.

Chapter Eighteen

"Nibbles!" I gasped as the naughty rabbit popped his head out from under the seat. "You were supposed to stay at the villa!"

I was so surprised, it took me a moment to realize I had spoken out loud in Rabbit language. Luckily everyone in the coach was still singing. Other than Esme, Knox was the only person who could hear me. But he had a shock of his own. At exactly the same moment I was shouting at Nibbles, Smoky hopped on to his boot.

"Whoa! Hello, long ears! How did you get in the coach?" Knox blinked with surprise as he stared at the little grey bunny sitting on his foot.

"Desperate demons!" I groaned as Esme nudged me in the ribs. She pointed to Bunnykins the Second hopping down the aisle. The twins had scooped up Cozy and Dozy and were cuddling them in their laps. Speckles was twitching her nose and sitting beside Smoky on Knox's other boot. Midnight, shy as ever, had darted under the back seat. I could see Fluffy's long hair poking out from there too.

"It's only me and a couple friends," said Nibbles, talking in Rabbit language which probably sounded to everyone else as if he was clicking his teeth. "We hopped back into the coach while the driver was dozing.

The others didn't want to come."

A couple of friends? It was more than that. I began to count, expecting to find the whole gang of naughty bunnies we had named:

1. Nibbles (the greedy leader, of course)
2. Bunnykins the Second
   (sitting with Esme)
3. Smoky (on Knox's right boot)
4. Speckles (on Knox's left boot)
5. Cozy (on Zoe's lap)
6. Dozy (on Zac's lap)
7. Midnight (under the back seat)
8. Fluffy (under the seat as well)

Hold on! There were three were missing:

9. Ginger (?)
10. Chocolate (?)
11. Snowy (?)

Perhaps they were on the coach somewhere.

"We have to do something! Esme and I wanted to get the rabbits away from Merrymeet before they were captured," I said, trying to explain everything to Knox and the twins as simply as I could (without mentioning magic). "We smuggled them on to the coach and set them free in the woods – but some came back..."

I was taking a risk — I didn't know for sure if I could trust Knox not to tell anyone. After all, it was his Uncle Bruiser who was trying to trap the rabbits for Mr Seymour. But right now, I had no choice. He had two bunnies sitting on his enormous boots.

Although we were in the back row and nobody else had spotted the rabbits yet, it wouldn't be long before somebody turned around. "We can't let anyone see them," I whispered. "Not Miss Marker or the coach driver because they might make us hand them over to the village authorities."

"You mean to Mr Seymour!" added Esme.

"Exactly. And we can't tell Piers, of course. The less people who know, the better."

"Right. We need to hide them," said

Zoe, gently lifting Cozy inside her school sweatshirt.

Zac took Dozy. And Esme did the same with Bunnykins the Second.

"You have to keep out of sight," I said, scooping Nibbles up so that I could whisper into his long fluffy ear. "If only you'd stayed at the villa like I told you to."

"Not likely!" I felt Nibbles shiver in my arms. "I saw that poor Roman rabbit hanging up in the kitchen to go in a Roman rabbit pie."

"It wasn't real," I sighed. But it was too late to explain that now.

"Come on!" Knox picked up Smoky and Speckles as if they were tiny mice in his giant hands. He slipped one into each of his coat pockets. "There you go!" he said gently. I knew in that moment that I could trust him with the rabbits' lives.

"I think there's still three more... No, just two now," I said as Ginger poked his head out from the under the back seat. I bent right down towards him and whispered quickly in Rabbit language. "Stay there and tell Midnight and Fluffy not to move."

I hoped Chocolate and Snowy might be under there as well. But then I saw them. They were hopping down the aisle towards us. And Miss Marker was coming too.

She hadn't seen the bunnies yet, as she was leaning over the seats, collecting in the worksheets and making her way towards us at the back of the bus.

She had already reached Keeley and Lexie just two seats in front.

"Don't worry!" said Knox. He stuck out his legs as far as he could, stretching them along the aisle to try and hide the rabbits.

But Chocolate had other ideas. He shot

up Knox's left trouser leg as if it were a rabbit's burrow.

Whee! Snowy whizzed up the right leg.

"Yikes!" yelped Knox. "I wasn't expecting that!"

"Everything all right back here?" asked Miss Marker.

"Just perfect!" giggled the whole back row, handing her our worksheets as quickly as we could.

"That was a close one!" said Zoe as Miss Marker made her way back to the front of the bus.

"You can say that again!" Knox wriggled.

Now at least I knew where all eleven naughty bunnies were hiding.

"What are we going to do with them all when we get back to the village?" I said, turning to Esme.

But she was staring out of the window

with her mouth wide open.

I saw at once that we were passing the windmill.

"Look!" she cried. "It's Mr Seymour. He's come already!"

The meadow was full of bulldozers and

diggers and trucks. Mr Seymour himself was standing beside the windmill in a bright-yellow builder's hat. He was pointing to a crane with a giant metal wrecking ball swinging like an iron fist.

"He said we had six more days!" gasped Esme. She bundled Bunnykins the Second into my arms and leapt to her feet.

"Stop the coach!" she cried, running down the aisle. "Please! Stop the coach."

Chapter Nineteen

I think the coach driver must have thought Esme was going to be sick or something. He opened the door quicker than a wizard with a wand.

Esme was halfway across the meadow before Miss Marker caught up with her.

"Wait!" cried the desperate teacher. "You have to be careful with all this machinery around."

But the rest of the class were already

down the steps and in the meadow behind her.

"Aren't my dad's machines awesome?" boasted Piers. "They'll knock the windmill down in two seconds flat."

"Quick!" I whispered to my friends on the back row. "Leave the rabbits here. We have to help Esme."

As Knox and the twins dashed to the coach door, I lined the bunnies up under the back seat.

"You're in charge," I said to Ginger who always seemed the most sensible. "Don't let Nibbles lead you astray." I grabbed a bag of carrot sticks left over from my packed lunch. "Share these and stay here. Do you understand me?"

Eleven little bunnies nodded their heads. Even Nibbles looked like he meant it.

"Try and be good!" I said, and then I

ran down the aisle, almost colliding with
the driver as he stepped out of the coach
to see what was going on as well.

Everyone was crowded
around the windmill.
Mrs Lee was
standing on the
doorstep holding
baby Bean, who
was clutching his
yellow rabbit toy.
Gretel was peering
out from behind her
mum's skirt.

"Mr Seymour turned up an hour ago
with all these bulldozers and things,"
Mrs Lee told Esme. "I was trying to write
a story, so I didn't notice at first. Then
I looked out of the window and there
they all were."

"But surely Mr Seymour can't knock down the windmill just like that?" said Zoe.

"He'll need written permission from the council," said Zac.

Esme and I looked desperately at Miss Marker and the coach driver, hoping the adults would back this up.

"That's right! You need papers," nodded the driver. "My brother-in-law had to wait six months just to knock down his own garden shed."

Mr Seymour hadn't even waited six days.

"Dad's got all that stuff sorted," said Piers. "His friends in the council signed everything."

"My colleagues in the council, you mean," said Mr Seymour, appearing suddenly with Lady Trim beside him. "It was all very professional and above board. I went to see them again this morning to tell them I'd sort out the terrible rabbit plague that's been ravishing Merrymeet."

"Rabbit plague?" Mrs Lee looked confused.

But Mr Seymour carried on. "When Lady Trim and the council saw how helpful I was being, they said I could get on with building my concrete car park out here just as soon as I like."

"Well somebody had to do something," mumbled Lady Trim.

"Only because you're head of the Allotment Committee as well as the council!" said Esme bravely. "You just wanted the rabbits to stop eating your precious vegetables."

"I still don't understand what any of this has got to do with rabbits," said poor Mrs Lee in confusion.

But I knew it had all started when Nibbles bit Piers's nose. I only needed to see the horrid grin on his face to know this whole thing was his way of getting revenge on Esme. But it wasn't her fault, of course. It was mine.

"We're wasting time," snarled Mr Seymour. "I've got all the papers here." He waved a large brown envelope in the air. "Get these children out of the way, Miss Marker; I need to start knocking things down."

"I'd like to have a look at the papers first," said Miss Marker, holding her hand out towards Mr Seymour and Lady Trim as if she had caught them passing a naughty note in class.

"Oh, would you?" Mrs Lee's face lit up. "Just to check they seem fair. . ."

"Of course." Miss Marker nodded and Mr Seymour handed over the envelope with a scowl.

"I'll make us all a nice cup of tea . . . at least while I've still got a kitchen," said Mrs Lee.

"As long as you've got proper china teacups," sighed Lady Trim, following her inside.

"Send a cuppa out for me, Miss Marker. I'll keep an eye on the kids for you," said the coach driver. Half the class had already wandered off and were kicking a football about.

"Complete waste of time! The papers are in perfect order," growled Mr Seymour, but he followed the three women inside the windmill, leaving muddy footprints all across the hall.

His drivers climbed out of their trucks and diggers.

"This won't make any difference," groaned Esme. "As soon as Miss Marker reads those papers she'll realize that Merrymeet Council have found a way to let Mr Seymour build his horrid concrete car park right away.

They always agree to everything he wants."

"Unless there's bats, of course," said the coach driver.

"Bats? How would that help?" I asked.

"Doesn't have to be bats. Could be owls," said the driver. "That was the trouble when my brother-in-law wanted to knock down his shed. An environmental officer came from head office somewhere. He thought there might be some sort of rare bat living in the shed ... or was it an owl?" He chewed his lip thoughtfully. "Anyway, the point was, my brother-in-law wasn't allowed to knock down *anything* until they were absolutely sure there were no endangered creatures living there."

"And it had to be a bat or an owl?" I asked.

"I think it's the same for snakes," said the driver.

"Snakes?" This was getting better and better. I didn't know anything about council Persons or papers or environmental officers ... but I did know a lot about magical creatures like owls and bats and snakes.

"It's lizards and moths and beetles too," said Zoe knowledgeably.

"Lizards?" I was almost jumping about with excitement.

"Any kind of endangered species can stop building works if they are found to be living there," agreed Zac. "Natterjack toads are about the rarest of all."

"Toads!" Now I really did leap in the air. "I know all about them!"

There might be a way that I could save the windmill after all...

Chapter Twenty

My fingers curled around my pink fluffy wand. I couldn't turn back time or cast a spell to make Mr Seymour and his machines vanish, but perhaps there was a better way to get rid of him. If I could magically summon some sort of rare animal to come and live in the meadow then the environmental officer Person would send the diggers away and Mr Seymour wouldn't be allowed to build his horrid concrete car park after all. I was just about to speak, when—

"I've got an idea," said Zoe, drawing us away from the bulldozers. "We can call the environmental office and get them to send someone over here to look for endangered species at once. I bet there's *something* endangered around here."

"I can even ask my brother-in-law for the number if you like," said the coach driver.

"It's no good," sighed Esme. "I don't think there are any rare creatures in the meadow. I've only ever seen slugs and snails and a couple of pigeons."

"The slugs might be rare," said Zac hopefully.

"The important thing is to make sure Mr Seymour can't knock down the windmill today," said Zoe. "We can start a petition or something later. All we need is a little time. If we call the environmental office, at least that will slow things down."

"Exactly. You keep an eye on the machines," I told Knox who was towering over us. "Don't let anyone start knocking anything down until the twins have made their phone call."

"I'll say we've seen a natterjack toad," said Zac. "I know exactly what they look like. They have a big yellow stripe down their backs."

"Perfect! We'll head down to the stream at the bottom of the meadow and see what we can find," I said, beckoning Esme to follow me. I wanted to get her by herself to explain my secret magic part of the plan. But, as we ran past a giant bulldozer, Piers stepped out from behind it.

"Where are you off to?" He laughed nastily. "Are you going home, Esme? Oh, I forgot, you don't have a home do you?

Or not for much longer anyway?"

"I wish you could turn *him* into a natterjack toad," sighed Esme as we ignored him and ran on.

"I did think about it. Nothing would give me more pleasure than to turn Piers Seymour into a slimy reptile!" After all, this was his doing – asking his dad to punish Esme and getting rid of the rabbits too, all because he hated Nibbles. "But turning Persons into toads just because you don't like them is the sort of magic that will get us into trouble," I said firmly.

"So what *is* your plan?" asked Esme.

"You'll see," I said, crouching down on my hands and knees by the edge of the stream. "Ribbit..." I croaked. "Ribbit, Ribbit!"

I cocked my head and listened.

"That was Toad Talk," I explained to

Esme. "If there is a natterjack anywhere near, it will hear me and come running ... or hopping, anyway."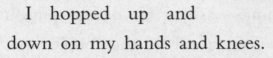

"You do look funny," smiled Esme.

I hopped up and down on my hands and knees.

"Ribbit! Ribbit!" I called desperately. "Please toads come and help us!"

Nothing happened. After fifteen minutes I gave up. "Maybe there aren't any toads near here," I sighed. I tried a little owl – "Twit-twoo!" – and bat – "Eeeeeeeeeeeeeeeeeeee!" – just in case that would work. Still nothing.

"The bats and owls will be sleeping. They won't come while it's daytime anyway," I sighed.

"If only we had our recorders," said Esme.

"Perhaps we could play a toad-charming tune."

We looked across the meadow. Zac and Zoe were waving to us from the gate by the road. A car had pulled in and they were talking to a woman wearing a long white coat.

"That must be the environmental officer already," groaned Esme.

"And we still haven't got a toad," I said. "If there are no endangered species here, Mr Seymour will be allowed to knock the windmill down and cover the meadow in concrete."

Esme was pacing by the side of the stream.

"Listen," she said. "I've had an idea. If there aren't any real toads and you won't turn horrible Piers Seymour into one, then how about me?"

"You?" I asked.

"Yes!" Esme hopped up and down. "Turn me into a toad! *Please!*"

"It's too dangerous," I gasped. "I accidentally turned Aunt Hemlock into a toad once. She insisted on hopping everywhere for a whole week afterwards. She wouldn't walk or ride her broomstick, and she kept sticking out her tongue and eating flies."

"But I'll know the spell is coming," said Esme bravely. "I'll close my eyes and think of all my favourite foods like cupcakes and marshmallows and chocolate. And I'll imagine myself running through the meadow. If I keep my memories with me, there won't be any chance of hopping about or eating flies when I turn back again."

"I'm not even sure I can do the spell properly. It was a mistake last time..."

"You have to try. It's our only chance to

save Windmill Meadow!" said Esme.

The environmental officer Person was walking through the orchard with the twins. I could hear Zoe saying loudly, "Um, yes, I think it was just over here that we saw the rare creature. . ."

Esme looked up at me and her blue eyes were full of hope. "Please," she begged. "I know you can do it, Bella. You're brilliant at magic."

"I suppose I could try," I said slowly. "I could turn you into a toad just for an hour or two."

"A rare natterjack toad," said Esme.

"All right. But we'll need to be quick." If I didn't act fast I would lose my nerve completely. "Ready? Just promise me you'll keep thinking about marshmallows and chocolate," I said as I began to mutter a spell.

*Take my friend and turn her
green...
Like the rarest natterjack ever seen!*

No sooner had I waved my wand than there was a puff of smoke.

Esme was gone. For a minute I thought she had vanished altogether.

"Esme? Where are you?" I cried.

"Ribbit!"

I looked down to see a tiny toad hopping up and down in the mud. It was no bigger than my hand with webbed feet, bendy knees, warty green skin, popping-out eyes and a thin yellow stripe down its back.

"Esme?" I said. "Is that you?"

"Ribbit!" she answered.

I really had turned my best friend into a toad.

Chapter Twenty-One

Esme hopped towards me.

Boing!

She was a perfect natterjack toad.

I bent down and scooped her up in my hands.

"Ooh, you are cold and slimy!" I giggled, almost dropping her by mistake.

"Thanks very much!" croaked Esme, answering in Toad Talk and blowing a big wet bubble at me.

"Come on! The environmental officer is still in the orchard," I said. But Esme started to wriggle. "Yikes! What are you doing?" She leapt right out of my hand.

"Sorry!" she croaked, jumping away. "It's being a toad ... I can't help myself. All I want to do is hop ... and I'm suddenly desperate for a swim!"

Boing! Boing! Boing!

"Stop!" I only just managed to grab her slimy webbed foot before she dived head first into the stream.

"Ribbit!" she stuck out her long, slippery tongue.

"You can't go swimming now. We have to save the windmill," I reminded her. Esme was starting to think far too much like a real toad. I opened my sleeve so that she could hide inside there. It would be safer than trying to hold her in my hand while she was so bouncy.

"Eeek!" I shivered as her slippery feet hopped along my arm. "Just don't go leaping about... Not till we see the environmental officer and I give you the word," I said, setting off towards the orchard. I couldn't wait to see the twins' faces when they saw I had a real natterjack toad. Zac had said that would save the windmill for sure.

I was running so fast I almost tripped over something in the grass ... something white and plump and fluffy.

"Nibbles?" I gasped as I stumbled forward. "Oh no! That's all we need!" The rabbits had escaped from the coach.

Nibbles was happily chewing a fallen apple while Snowy, Chocolate and Speckles all rolled around in the long grass. I saw a wisp of Fluffy's hair caught on a bush and a streak of grey as Smoky dashed past.

Midnight was cowering shyly behind a tree and Cosy and Dozy were just settling down for a nap.

At least they were keeping well away from the big machines. The environmental officer hadn't noticed them either. She was too busy tapping the bark of the trees.

Poor sensible Ginger popped his head out from under a bramble bush and clicked his teeth as if to say "Sorry!" I'd left him in charge but he hadn't managed to keep the other rabbits on the bus. I couldn't blame him. I knew how hard it was to control the naughty bunnies – especially when Nibbles was hungry and looking for food. He had eaten the fallen apple right down to the core and now his whiskers were covered in dark purple juice as he munched on a fat, ripe blackberry.

"Tumbling trolls! It's the whole gang

again," I groaned as Bunnykins the Second squeezed under the hedge. I opened my sleeve so that Esme could see her favourite rabbit hopping past.

"Ribbit!" she cried. But poor Bunnykins the Second looked startled and leapt away.

"We'll just have to worry about them later," I whispered, running on towards the environmental officer and the twins. "There's not a moment to lose. It's time for you to do your toad thing, Esme."

I sprinted across the orchard. "Excuse me," I called out as the officer reached one of the huge bulldozer digging machines. "I have found a rare natterjack toad."

"A natterjack?" The environmental officer shook her head. "You must be mistaken. Natterjack toads like sandy ground, not grassy meadows like this one. It would be most unusual to find a natterjack living here. It is quite the wrong habitat."

"Oh. . ." I stammered. "But. . ."

"Couldn't there be an exception?" asked Zac.

"Please, Dr Greenwood," Zoe joined in, grabbing the environmental officer by the arm. "Couldn't you just take a look? If there is a rare natterjack toad, the digging would have to stop, wouldn't it?"

"Well, yes. . ." Dr Greenwood pulled a notebook out of the pocket of her white coat.

"Ready, Esme," I whispered in Toad Talk, quickly shaking my sleeve. "Esme?"

I shook my sleeve again and peered inside it.

"Esme?" I croaked. But my sleeve was empty. She was gone.

Chapter Twenty-Two

The environmental officer stared at me as I fell to my knees and began desperately searching through the long grass. "There was a toad. Really there was," I promised.

"Back to work, everybody!" I heard Mr Seymour's voice booming across the meadow. He waved the brown envelope in the air as he stepped out of the windmill. Miss Marker stood in the doorway with her arm around Mrs Lee. Lady Trim followed with her head bowed in shame.

"Just like I said, these papers are all in order. Signed and sealed by the council!" Mr Seymour crowed. "Nothing can stop me covering this whole place in concrete."

"There's nothing I can do either," Dr Greenwood told me and the twins apologetically. "I wish there was. This is such a beautiful place. But there is no sign of any endangered species."

"But there really was a natterjack. I saw it too," said Zoe, scrabbling around in the grass beside me.

"Did you?" I turned towards her. If she had seen a toad it must be Esme. "Thank goodness for that!"

"I'm only fibbing!" she whispered. "Just like you are. It's our last chance to save the windmill."

"But I'm not fibbing! You don't understand.

There really was a toad," I groaned as the giant machines above us began to rumble. I was afraid of something even more terrible than losing the windmill now. There was no sign of Esme. She could be anywhere, hopping around in the grass. She was so small the Persons driving the machines wouldn't notice her – and even if they did, they would only see a tiny toad. I couldn't imagine Mr Seymour's workers stopping for that.

The great digger beside us shuddered and sprang into life.

"Hurry, Indigo Class – come with me! It is not safe with all these machines," cried Miss Marker.

"Get digging!" bellowed Mr Seymour, above the roar of the engines. "Start in the orchard and bulldoze the trees."

"Stop!" I begged, waving my hands

wildly in the air. Wherever Esme was, she could be squashed at any moment.

"Move out of the way, little girl," yelled Mr Seymour. "I want this whole place covered in concrete by nightfall!"

"No!" I stepped out in front of the smallest apple tree and spread my arms wide. "I'm not going anywhere! I'm not moving!" I said.

The digger rolled towards me.

Chapter Twenty-Three

I have seen fierce fiery dragons and roaring mountain ogres back in the Magic Realm, but nothing was as terrifying as that enormous snarling machine with its terrible iron jaws.

"Out of the way!" cried the driver. I saw that it was Knox's Uncle Bruiser.

I was so scared, my whole body was shaking like a rattling skeleton. But I didn't move. I stayed rooted to the spot, right in front of the little apple tree with my arms spread out.

"You can't touch this orchard," I yelled. "Or the meadow. Or the windmill." I couldn't let the enormous digger move even another centimetre. If it rolled forward it might squash Esme. She had to be near here somewhere.

"Oh dear!" shrieked Lady Trim. "This has all gone a bit too far!"

"Bella! What are you doing?" cried Miss Marker, running towards me from the other side of the meadow.

Dr Greenwood stepped forward and took my arm, bravely standing beside me in front of the juddering machine. "You really do have to come away now," she shouted over the noise.

"But the toad... She's here somewhere. She's my best friend," I cried.

"Your best friend?" Dr Greenwood smiled. "I know what you mean," she said. "Some of my best friends are slimy creatures too. Snakes and snails. Even slugs . . . I love them all."

"You don't understand," I said, realizing I would have to confess everything, even if meant telling everybody I was a witch. I couldn't let Esme be squashed to death. "She's not really a toad, you see. . ."

"Well, she's almost certainly not a natterjack," interrupted Dr Greenwood kindly. "As I explained, this isn't the right habitat at all. Meadow grass like this is much more suited to rabbits or deer or—"

"Rabbits?" Suddenly I knew what I had to do. "Stop!" I bellowed, throwing my arms in the air again. "You can't bulldoze the meadow. There are rare bunnies living here."

"Rare bunnies?" said Dr Greenwood.

"Where?"

The giant metal teeth of the machine snapped and shuddered above us but I stood my ground and pointed to the bramble hedge. "There!" Nibbles poked his head out from under a bush. His pink nose was bright purple with blackberry juice.

"Turn off the engines!" cried Dr Greenwood, grabbing her notebook.

"Yes! Turn them off at once!" cried Miss Marker, skidding to a stop beside us. Most of Indigo Class were right behind her. "Bella, are you all right?" She scooped me into a hug. "You were so brave," she said (and it was better than any gold star she could ever have given me). "But also very silly. You can't just stand in front of a dangerous machine like this. You scared me!"

"I'm sorry!" I flushed as hot as a boiling cauldron. I was glad she was still holding on to me as my knees felt so weak I almost fell over. The rattling engine of the giant digger shuddered to a halt at last.

The children cheered.

I looked around, desperately trying to see Esme, but there was still no sign of the tiny toad.

"Bunny rabbits?" Bruiser Bailey climbed down from the giant digger. He shook his fist as Dr Greenwood. "You can't make us stop work because of a few bunny rabbits."

"There's nothing special about these rabbits," agreed Mr Seymour, thundering across the orchard to join us. "Best thing we could do is put them in a pie. There's been a plague of the long-eared leapers all over Merrymeet Village."

"Not any more! Most of them are safe at the Roman villa now!" whispered Zoe, squeezing my hand.

"Set some traps, Bruiser," said Mr Seymour, clicking his fingers as Snowy and Speckles poked their heads up in the long grass beside Nibbles. "Better still, fetch a gun. We'll deal with this lot in no time."

"No!" I cried. "You can't. These rabbits are rare and magical and—"

"They're just bunnies!" said Mr Seymour, clicking his fingers again. "Get on with it Bruiser."

"Not so fast!" said Dr Greenwood. "There does seem to be something very unusual about these rabbits."

Mr Seymour's shouting must have frightened Nibbles and the gang. All we could see was a row of fluffy bottoms poking up in the air as the rabbits tried to dig a burrow and escape.

Even Cozy and Dozy had woken up and were digging too. We could see eleven tails all in a row ... and each little tail had a magic star on it.

"Extraordinary! I have never seen markings like that before," said Dr Greenwood, almost dancing a jig, she was so excited. "These rabbits could be extremely rare. A whole new breed perhaps." She picked a clump of Fluffy's hair from a nearby bramble bush and popped it into a little plastic bag. "All work in this meadow will have to stop while I investigate."

"You mean Mr Seymour can't build his car park?" I asked. "The windmill will be safe? And the meadow too?"

"The machines will never be allowed back again if these rabbits really are as rare and special as they look," said Dr Greenwood.

Ginger poked his head out from behind

a tree. "There's no magic rabbits like us in the whole of the Person World," he said wisely in Rabbit language. Then he clicked his teeth and winked at me.

"Oh these rabbits are rare … and very special. I am sure of it," I said. I was tingling all over with excitement. If only I could find Esme and share the good news.

"Three cheers for Bella," whooped Zac. "The diggers would never have stopped if she hadn't spotted the bunnies hiding in the grass."

"Hip, hip, hooray!" cheered Indigo Class (or most of them anyway). Piers looked furious, of course, and Malinda and Fay took his side as usual.

Knox cheered louder than anybody else. "Three cheers for the rabbits too!" he called. I always knew he was good and kind really. "I love bunnies," he whispered in my ear. "When I was told to set the traps I made sure they wouldn't really go off." Then he blushed bright red as his Uncle Bruiser grabbed him by the ear and marched him towards the digger.

"You haven't heard the last of this," said Mr Seymour, jabbing his finger at Mrs Lee. "I . . . I'll appeal to the council . . . I'll—"

"I think you'll find," Lady Trim said haughtily, "that any – ah – arrangement you might have with the council is off. You said you would get rid of the rabbits, and you've obviously failed. Goodbye, Mr Seymour." She swept off angrily.

Mrs Lee straightened her spectacles. "Yes, hop along Mr Seymour and take your machines with you! The Rabbits of Windmill Meadow have won this battle," she said firmly. Then she passed baby Bean to Gretel and flung her arms around my neck.

"Thank you, Bella! We could never have stopped Mr Seymour's machines without you," she said. "But where's Esme? She'll jump for joy when she hears the good news. . ."

All I could think about was Esme jumping like a toad.

"Er . . . I'll try and find her," I said, staring hopelessly at the ground.

We might have saved the windmill, but how could I explain to Mrs Lee that I had turned her daughter into a toad?

Chapter Twenty-Four

What if my tiny slimy best friend had already been squashed by one of the terrible diggers? What if, what if — it was all too awful to think about.

"Where are you, Esme?" I groaned. I closed my eyes and tried to imagine where I would hop off to if I was a toad. "Leaping lobsters! Of course!"

I sped off across the meadow. "I know where she is... I'm going to find Esme!"

I called.

"Quick as you can, Bella. I want everyone back on the coach in five minutes," Miss Marker shouted after me.

"We'll be there," I promised. *At least I hope we will*, I thought, clutching my wand as I skidded to a stop beside the stream.

I remembered how desperate Esme had been to go for a swim... If she had escaped the diggers and gone anywhere, then surely it would be here.

"Yes!" I clapped my hands as I saw a trail of tiny toad prints in the mud. "Esme!" I cried, spotting her at the edge of the stream. But it was too late. She dived head first into the water.

Plop!

Her little webbed feet disappeared below the surface.

"Wait!" I called. If Esme swam downstream I would never be able to find her again.

I waded into the shallow water and began paddling towards her.

"Esme, come back!" I rolled my sleeves up and plunged my hands right down to the mud at the bottom of the stream – just the sort of place a toad would love to squelch about. "Got you!" I cried, grabbing something wet and slippery, but it was only a piece of weed.

Then I heard a big wet *PLOP* as she leapt out of the water just ahead of me.

I plunged forward, tripped over a stone and fell *SPLAT!* in the stream.

I looked like a dripping–wet marsh monster as I clambered to my feet covered from head to toe in mud and weeds and slime.

The stream was all stirred up like a swirling cauldron and there was no sign of Esme anywhere.

"Where are you?" I cried in despair.

Then I felt something hopping about amongst the slimy weeds on top of my head.

"Is that you?" I asked, nearly leaping out of my skin as Esme sprung past the end of my muddy nose and plopped into my outstretched palm.

"At last!" I cried, holding her firmly in one hand and wiping the other on the clean grass at the edge of the stream. "I thought you'd been squashed by the diggers!"

I grabbed my soggy wand and waved it over Esme's head.

Little toad you've had your fun,
But now your hopping days
are done.
You must turn back to a girl,
When I give my wand a
twir . . . . l!

Esme shot up to full size so quickly we both tumbled into the stream again.

Splosh!

"Slithering serpents!" I cried as the wet, pink wand flew out of my slippery fingers.

It spun through the air just as Piers Seymour appeared over the hill.

"What are you two up to now?" he scowled.

Bam!

The wand hit him right on the top of his head.

"Ouch!" he yelped. "What was that? And why are you two sitting in the stream?"

Before we could answer his questions there was a faint puff of green smoke.

Piers looked startled for a moment. Then, to my amazement, he crouched down and started hopping around at the edge of the water.

Boing! Boing! Boing!

"Oh dear!" When the wand hit Piers a tiny bit of the toad magic must have been left on the end of it. Esme and I looked at each other, trying not to laugh. "It really was an accident!" I whispered, helping her to her feet. "And at least Piers hasn't turned green or slimy or anything. But I think he might be hopping like that for a few days yet."

"Serves him right for throwing my family out of our windmill!" said Esme.

"Laughing lizards! You didn't hear the good news," I cried, realizing she must have set off to the stream before the diggers were stopped. "The concrete car park can't be built. Dr Greenwood saw the magic rabbits. She says they are really rare. As long as the bunnies live in the meadow, there is nothing Piers or his father can do."

"You mean . . . you saved the windmill?" cried Esme, flinging her muddy arms around me. "You did it! You actually did it!"

"*We* did it!" I laughed. "You and me and the bunnies. The twins too. Even Knox. Everyone helped in their own way."

"All except Piers!" Esme scowled at him

as he hopped past.

Piers stuck out his tongue and swallowed a fly.

"Eww! That's even more disgusting than eating Brussels sprouts," I giggled.

Piers kept bouncing (and eating flies) for the next two weeks.

Whenever he saw me and Esme at school he croaked insults at us under his breath, but he couldn't prove we had anything to do with his strange behaviour or the way the rabbits had magically appeared in time to stop the car park being built.

By the time Piers's toady ways finally wore off, Mr Seymour's diggers had left Windmill Meadow for good. A sign on the gate said:

RARE RABBITS!
PROTECTED SITE.

Dr Greenwood wrote a letter to the council confirming scientific tests had discovered Nibbles and his friends were unique. No building or digging would be allowed in the meadow so long as the rare rabbits lived there.

Miss Marker called for an investigation, and it turned out the documents saying Esme's great-grandfather sold the land to the Seymours had been faked too. All of Mr Seymour's friends had to resign from the council. Lady Trim didn't seem to mind too much.

"I want more time for gardening," she said. "The bunnies have somewhere lovely outside the village to live and the allotments are safe at last."

So it was a happy ending for everyone! Especially Esme and her family.

"This really is our home now and the bunnies can stay for ever too!" she told me when I came to the windmill for tea.

"Of course they can!" Mrs Lee looked up from her notebook and smiled. "And I've had an idea for a story at last," she explained as we peered over her shoulder.

THE BUNNIES
OF WINDMILL
MEADOW

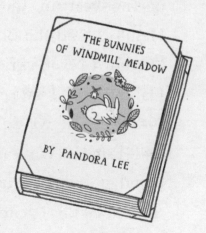

BY
PANDORA LEE.

"I haven't seen Mum as happy as this for a long time!" Esme whispered.

"Come on!" I smiled as we tiptoed away. "Let's go and see how the rabbits have settled into their new home."

"Good idea. I want to check Nibbles isn't eating everything in the pumpkin patch," said Esme. "I'm saving the biggest pumpkin to make a lantern for Halloween."

"Halloween?" I skidded to a stop. Halloween was always the scariest night of the year in the Magic Realm. Aunt Hemlock and the other witches went wild. "I didn't even know Persons celebrated Halloween," I said with a shiver.

"Of course we do. It's the best fun ever," said Esme. "We can go trick or treating together and dress up and. . ." Suddenly she snorted with excited laughter. "You can come as a witch!"

"If only I still had my pointy hat," I giggled as she grabbed my hand and we ran on across the meadow together.

"It's going to be so much fun. I know I can't do real magic," said Esme, "but maybe you could teach me to ride a broomstick!"

"Of course I will," I agreed, with a wave of my fluffy pink wand.

"Promise?" asked Esme.

"Best friend promise!" I said.

Acknowledgements

So many of the magic folk at Scholastic
have cast spells to help bring Bella to life.
Thanks to you all! A special wand wave
to my brilliant editor Genevieve Herr,
eagle-eyed Pete Matthews, Samuel Perrett
for design, Olivia Horrox, Jade Tolley and
all the publicity, rights and sales teams.
Also Claire Wilson and Rosie Price at
RCW. And Sophie McKenzie for our
monthly broomstick rides!